THE PUPPY EXPRESS

BOOKS IN THE PUPPY PATROL™ SERIES

COMING SOON

THE PUPPY EXPRESS

JENNY DALE

Illustrations by Mick Reid
Cover illustration by Michael Rowe

AN
APPLE
PAPERBACK

SCHOLASTIC INC.
New York Toronto London Auckland Sydney
Mexico City New Delhi Hong Kong Buenos Aires

SPECIAL THANKS TO LORNA READ

No part of this publication may be reproduced, in whole or in part, or stored in a
retrieval system, or transmitted in any form or by any means, electronic,
mechanical, photocopying, recording, or otherwise, without written permission
of the publisher. For information regarding permission, please
write to Macmillan Publishers Ltd., 20 New Wharf Rd.,
London N1 9RR Basingstoke and Oxford.

ISBN 0-439-45355-0

All rights reserved. Published by Scholastic Inc., 557 Broadway,
New York, NY 10012 by arrangement with Macmillan Children's Books,
a division of Macmillan Publishers Ltd.

SCHOLASTIC and associated logos are trademarks and/or registered trademarks
of Scholastic Inc.

12 11 10 9 8 7 6 5 4 3 2 1   3 4 5 6 7 8/0

Printed in the U.S.A.   40
First Scholastic printing, August 2003

CHAPTER ONE

"**S**low down, Jake!" called Neil Parker as his young Border collie raced ahead to greet an older dog, barking excitedly.

Neil and his ten-year-old sister, Emily, followed Jake down the path that led to the Compton Station railroad tracks, where a magnificent old steam engine was gleaming in the sun.

"Hello, Skip." Neil bent down and stroked the older dog's silky black head as Jake greeted Skip eagerly. Skip was Jake's uncle, and the two dogs were always happy to see each other.

A plump, friendly looking man who had been crouching beside the engine with a paintbrush in his hand, straightened up as he heard them approach.

"Hi, Jim," called Neil.

"Hello, you two," replied signalman Jim Brewster. "Hello, Jake." He laughed as he watched the Border collies rolling around together playfully.

"How's it going?" Emily asked.

"Oh, fine," said Jim. "But I could use a few more days to get Old Bessie ready for her first trip on Sunday. The gold paint I ordered should be arriving tomorrow. Then I'll be able to paint your name at last, won't I, girl?"

"It's looking great already," said Neil, admiring the black-and-red paintwork that gleamed in the mid-June sun.

Jim gave the side of the engine a pat, as if it were a dog. "You should have seen Bessie when we first got her," he said. "She was a heap of rust. The steam train club has put months of work into restoring her, and Councillor Jepson has given us some funds — on the condition that we let Old Bessie be used for tourist rides, too."

Neil and Emily admired the giant locomotive, while Jake and Skip raced past in a noisy game of chase. Old Bessie was much bigger than a modern electric train — her iron wheels were almost as tall as Neil. There was a big funnel at the front, and a cab containing the controls. To get into the cab, you had to climb up two steps and push open a pair of waist-high swinging doors.

Neil had only seen steam engines in old films, and

he couldn't wait to see Old Bessie in motion. With just a few more touches, she would be ready. And her first trip was for such a good cause, too. The proceeds would go toward a memorial to a brave dog who had once lived in Compton. That was why Neil and Emily had decided to be involved right from the start.

"We've come to see if we can have some more tickets to sell for the Puppy Express trip," said Emily.

"You two are doing well," said Jim. "How many have you sold by now? Sixteen, is it?"

"Nineteen, actually," Emily told him. "Mostly to people visiting the kennel."

Bob and Carole Parker, Neil and Emily's parents, ran King Street Kennels, a boarding kennel and rescue center in the busy market town of Compton. The Parker family were known as the Puppy Patrol because of all the work they did for dogs.

"Do you have those leaflets you promised us? It's getting a little late to hand them out now," said Neil, frowning.

"There's been a problem at the printer's — it's their computer system," explained Jim. "But it's fixed now, so they should be in tomorrow — or even later today. Why don't you come by here after school tomorrow and pick some up?"

"Sure," said Neil. "I don't suppose we could have a guided tour of the engine at the same time?" he added hopefully.

"I'll see," Jim said, his weather-beaten face breaking into a broad grin. "Come on — the tickets are locked in a safe in the station."

"Jake!" called Neil. The black-and-white collie looked around, then raced toward Neil, with Skip trotting beside him. The two lively dogs ran ahead as everyone headed for the station building.

"How many tickets are left?" asked Emily.

"About forty," replied Jim.

"But that's a lot," said Neil anxiously.

"Don't worry." Jim laughed. "I'm sure there'll be a big demand for tickets on the day of the trip. We're running two coaches, each holding thirty people and their dogs, and I bet every place will be taken."

"I can't wait!" said Neil. He imagined the magnificent steam train full of dogs of every shape and size. It really would be a fantastic day.

Jim unlocked the safe and counted out a dozen tickets for them. Then he whistled for Skip and said good-bye, eager to get back to Old Bessie.

As Neil and Emily left the station with Jake, Neil looked up and frowned. "I thought there were supposed to be posters up, advertising the trip," he said to Emily. "It doesn't seem very well organized, does it?"

"What do you expect, with Mrs. Jepson involved?" Emily said with a shrug. "She can't even organize her dogs, let alone a train ride!"

"Yeah, it's a pity she ever got involved in the first place," Neil grumbled. "But I suppose they *had* to make her chairperson of the committee, seeing as Mr. Jepson helped raise funds to restore the train — hey, look who's coming, Em! Let's see if she wants to buy a ticket!"

Neil had spotted Jane Hammond driving up to the station. Jane was the owner of Jake's mother, Delilah, and she and her husband Richard owned Old Mill Farm.

Emily rushed up with a ticket as Jane parked and got out of her car.

"Hmm. What exactly is this Puppy Express?" she asked, looking at the ticket Emily held out to her.

"It's a special steam train trip for people and their dogs. It's for a good cause," Emily explained.

Neil and Jake caught up with Emily. Jake gave a little whine, eager for some attention. "What's the good cause?" Jane asked as she bent down to stroke the collie.

"Have you ever heard of a dog called Bessie, who lived in Compton during the Second World War?" asked Neil.

Jane shook her head. "That's a bit before my time!" she joked. "But tell me about her anyway."

Neil knew that he had caught her attention. Like him, she was always interested in anything to do with dogs.

"You know Mrs. Maitland-Smith, who lives at Honeybourne House?" he said.

"The horsey woman with the snooty voice?" asked Jane.

"Yes, that's the one," confirmed Neil. "She's got a black poodle called Jemima who sometimes boards with us. It was Mrs. Maitland-Smith's grandparents who owned Bessie. They went to visit relatives in Manchester during the war and the air-raid sirens went off in the night. They were all fast asleep, so nobody heard them —"

"Except for Bessie," put in Emily. "She barked and woke everyone up, and they got to the air-raid shelter just before a bomb dropped on the house. They all would have been killed if it hadn't been for Bessie."

"What a heroine! She must have been really de-

voted to her owners. What type of dog was she?" Jane asked.

"A golden retriever," said Neil. "It was Jim Brewster's idea to put up a memorial for her. And it was his idea to name the steam engine after her. Jim's mom used to be housemaid to Mrs. Maitland-Smith's grandparents at Honeybourne House. She told Jim about Bessie when he was little and he never forgot the story."

"Marcus Welham has agreed to cut the ribbon and officially name the engine on Sunday," said Emily.

"Will he bring Amber?" asked Jane.

Marcus Welham was the biggest soccer star the Compton area had ever produced. He had adopted an Airedale-cross pup named Amber from King Street Kennels.

"I think so. She's doing really well," said Emily. "She's been coming to Dad's obedience classes."

"Well, it sounds like fun and it's for a very good cause, too." Jane delved in her bag for her purse. "I'll take two tickets, please."

"Will you bring Delilah?" asked Emily.

"Of course!" Jane laughed.

"Great! I'm sure Jake will enjoy spending some time with his mom," said Neil, ruffling the collie's fur.

"Hello, Jim, how are you?" Jane Hammond called as Jim emerged from the station building.

"Exhausted!" The signalman mopped his brow

with an oily handkerchief. "And fed up," he added. "I can't find my stencils anywhere."

"What stencils?" asked Neil.

"The ones I had specially made to paint Old Bessie's name. I have no idea where I put them — oh, no! Just what I need!" he groaned.

A white Volvo was pulling up. A flurry of barks came from within, and as soon as the door was opened, two West Highland terriers leaped out. Their white fur was immaculate, and between each set of perky ears was a bow — pink for Sugar and blue for Spice. Jake ran to meet them, his tail wagging in friendly greeting. He remembered the terriers from their frequent stays at King Street Kennels.

The Westies' owner, a plump, middle-aged woman in a very short dress, smiled broadly. "Hello, everyone," she called cheerily. Her blond hair hung in ringlets and her face was covered with bright makeup.

"Hello, Mrs. Jepson," said Neil. "Sugar and Spice are looking well." Neil didn't approve of the way Mrs. Jepson took care of her dogs. She spoiled them rotten and didn't train them properly, so the two little Westies were very badly behaved. They were King Street's least favorite clients.

"My babies are wonderful, aren't you, darlings?" Mrs. Jepson cooed, scooping them up in her arms and rubbing her face against their fur. "Now, Jim, I want to have a chat with you about the arrangements for Sunday," she continued, adopting a brisk tone.

"I'll be on my way now," said Jane Hammond quickly. "I just stopped by for a summer train schedule."

"We'll see you on Sunday then, won't we?" Mrs. Jepson said to her. "Sugar and Spice are Old Bessie's mascots, you know. There'll be lots of photographers there. You never know, perhaps they'll squeeze your Delilah into a picture."

Jane Hammond raised her eyebrows and walked off with a wave. Neil and Emily exchanged a look. Mrs. Jepson was just impossible! Now she had started pestering poor Jim about the coaches. "It's not too late to alter the paintwork, is it, Jim? I just think that pink would look so much nicer with the blue upholstery."

"We've used the original colors," he said patiently. "We want the train to look as authentic as possible."

"Hmm, I suppose so," Mrs. Jepson said uncertainly. "Where will I be sitting with my lovely doggies? We want to make sure everyone gets a good view of my little beauties," she said, brightening up as she scurried after him into the station.

"Come on, Em, let's escape while we have the chance." Neil laughed. "Jake! Here, boy." He patted his leg and Jake left the post he was sniffing and ran back obediently to Neil's side. Neil bent down to clip on his leash.

"Look, here comes Jemima and Mrs. Maitland-Smith," said Emily. A tall woman was striding toward them, elegantly dressed in well-cut riding pants and highly polished leather boots. Trotting beside her was a poodle, its black fur in a fancy pom-pom cut.

"Poor dog," muttered Neil. "I hate to see poodles trimmed like that. It's so unnatural."

Emily nodded in agreement. "Hello, Mrs. Maitland-Smith," she said.

"Hello. Have you seen Jim Brewster anywhere?" she asked in her clipped accent.

"He's in there with —" began Neil, but before he could finish, Sugar and Spice ran out of the station, yapping excitedly, with Mrs. Jepson hurrying after them.

"Oh, hello!" said Mrs. Jepson, with exaggerated politeness.

Mrs. Maitland-Smith ignored her and, with a look of disdain, swept back to her car and snapped her fingers at Jemima. The poodle obediently jumped in beside her, and the car sped away, leaving Mrs. Jepson gaping in its wake.

"*Well!*" Mrs. Jepson said, still staring after the car. "How rude!"

"What was that all about?" Emily whispered to Neil.

Neil shrugged. "No clue," he replied. "But I think we'd better find out. It looks like those two have had some sort of fight. We don't want Sunday spoiled — if Mrs. Jepson and Mrs. Maitland-Smith are at each other's throats, you never know what might happen!"

CHAPTER TWO

"Going out, Neil?" Bob Parker was staring at his reflection in the hall mirror as Neil walked past the following day. He stroked his dark, bushy beard, then turned to Neil with a thoughtful expression. "Maybe it's time this beard went, since it's so hot. What do you think?" he asked.

Neil grinned. "I wouldn't shave it off now, Dad. I'd wait till winter," he said.

"Why?" asked Bob, looking puzzled.

"Do you really want a snow-white chin when the rest of your face is tan?" Neil laughed. "I'm off to check on the pups in the rescue center."

One of the rescue dogs, a pretty mongrel called Rusty, had given birth to four puppies two weeks ago. Their eyes were open now and the tiny crea-

tures were already developing individual personalities. Neil would have spent all day with them if he could. He was keeping a special eye on the smallest pup. She didn't seem to be developing as fast as her brothers, and Neil was worried about her.

"Hello, girl," he said, stroking Rusty gently and watching as the puppies fought for the best nursing position. The three male pups squeezed their small sister out, so Neil reached in between them and made a space for her. He watched as she sucked away, her eyes closed and her tail twitching in bliss. *Perhaps this is a regular problem,* he thought. *Maybe she isn't getting enough milk.* He made a mental note to mention it to his mom.

Neil left the puppies to feed and headed back to the

house. Jake was sleeping beside the kitchen door. He raised his head, pricked his ears, and thumped his tail. Neil knew exactly what he wanted.

"OK, boy. Let's go and get some exercise," he said.

"Don't be too long," called Carole from the kennel's office as she heard him go out. "You've got homework to do, remember?"

"All right," Neil agreed reluctantly.

Instead of taking Jake up to the park, he decided to go into Compton and stop by Jim's. He was eager to see if the leaflets about the train trip were ready, so that he and Emily could start handing them out.

Neil found Jim watering his front lawn. Skip was barking and playing in the spray from the sprinkler, and Jake ran to join him.

"Hi, Jim," called Neil. "Glad you managed to escape from Mrs. Jepson!"

"It wasn't easy, I can tell you!" The signalman grinned.

"Are the leaflets here yet?" asked Neil.

Jim shook his head. "I'm afraid not," he said. "It'll be tomorrow morning now, I imagine."

"Cut it out, Jake!" Neil laughed as the collie ran up to him and shook himself violently, showering Neil with cold water. Skip padded over to a bush and lay down under it, but the younger dog wouldn't rest. He kept running up to Skip, trying to get him to join in the game.

"I'll stop by the station after school, then," Neil

said. "With any luck, Mrs. Jepson won't be there. By the way, any idea what's going on between her and Mrs. Maitland-Smith?"

Jim sighed. "I don't know what's got into those two. Mrs. Maitland-Smith thinks she should be in charge of organizing everything instead of Mrs. Jepson — after all, Bessie did belong to her family. Plus, she thinks Jemima should be Old Bessie's mascot, not Sugar and Spice."

"Surely Mrs. Jepson could let Mrs. Maitland-Smith help her?" Neil said reasonably.

"That was the agreement, but you know Mrs. Jepson," said Jim. "She likes to have a finger in every pie. She was supposed to hand over the publicity to Mrs. Maitland-Smith, who probably would have done a very good job."

"Yeah!" Neil agreed. "She would have gotten a lot of interest from the press because of her family's connection — and because the engine is named after her grandmother's dog."

"I'm fed up with being piggy-in-the-middle." Jim sighed. "As soon as Mrs. Jepson tells me to do one thing, Mrs. Maitland-Smith tells me to do the opposite. So I do the only thing anyone could do — try to ignore the pair of them!"

"Stop that, Jake!" Neil called. Jake, who had started to dig a hole in a flower bed, looked up guiltily. "Did you find your stencils?" Neil asked Jim.

"No. And they're not the only things that have

gone missing. Either I'm going crazy, or there's a gremlin at work, making things disappear."

"Maybe you're working so hard that you can't remember where you've put things. I do that with my homework sometimes!" Neil grinned. "But they don't seem to believe me at school . . ." He whistled to Jake. "Good luck. See you tomorrow," he called, and set off back to King Street with Jake at his heel.

At assembly in Meadowbank School the next morning, Mr. Hamley, the principal, made a special announcement. "Mrs. Sharpe has asked me to help her find a home for a puppy," he said.

Neil nudged his friend Hasheem Lindon, but Hasheem was so wrapped up in what Mr. Hamley was saying that he didn't seem to notice.

Mrs. Sharpe was Neil and Hasheem's homeroom teacher. Mr. Hamley went on to explain that her next-door neighbor, Pauline Ford, had an English springer spaniel called Poppy. Poppy had had five pups, four of which had found homes. But nobody seemed to want the fifth.

At this point in his announcement, Mr. Hamley paused, and got what he expected — a chorus of *aahs*.

"Mrs. Sharpe tells me that the pup is a lively little brown-and-white female with a speckled nose and a white star on her forehead," the principal continued. "She's ready to leave now, but —" he held up a hand to silence the school as people started to talk and put their hands up "— I must warn you that anyone who's interested in adopting this pup should get their parents' permission first. And you should all remember that animals are a huge responsibility — you can't just send them back when you're fed up with them. If you're interested, come and see me. Now I've got some information about cricket practice. . . ."

Neil stopped listening. Cricket had never been his favorite sport. Anyway, it was impossible to concentrate on anything else Mr. Hamley was saying when he was feeling so angry. He managed to keep his feelings to himself until the end of the assembly, when they finally boiled over.

"What's wrong with the dogs and pups in our rescue center? They all need good homes, too," he said angrily to his best friends, Chris Wilson and Hasheem.

Before either of them had a chance to respond, Emily rushed up to join them.

"It's not fair!" she complained. "I wish Mr. Hamley would mention some of our dogs."

"Have you tried asking him?" Chris suggested.

Emily sighed. "It wouldn't do any good, really. It's an ongoing thing, you see. We get dogs and pups in all the time. Mr. Hamley would be making announcements every week, and there aren't that many people at school who want to adopt a dog."

"I know two people who would," said Hasheem.

Neil stared at him in surprise. "Who?" he asked.

"Rehana and me." Rehana was Hasheem's sister. She was in the same class as Neil and Emily's five-year-old sister, Sarah.

"Hey! We've got a litter of pups in the rescue center right now," Neil suggested hopefully. "They'll be ready to go to homes in six weeks. They're part Irish setter. They'd make great pets."

Hasheem shook his head. "Sorry," he said. "It's got to be a springer spaniel for us."

"Why?" Neil asked curiously. He was always interested in why certain people chose certain breeds of dog.

"Because springer spaniels *spring*!" joked Chris.

"That's right, they do!" Hasheem laughed. "My cousin's got one called Brandy, and he leaps around all over the place. Springers are great dogs. They've got lots of energy, and they're really smart and easy to train. Brandy can do tons of tricks. He balances things on his nose, then catches them in his mouth, he fetches the papers and the mail —"

"Hey, slow down!" Neil laughed. "I don't think you should expect Mrs. Ford's puppy to do all that right away. Springer pups can be very destructive. She's more likely to tear anything made of paper to shreds!"

"This is the first springer spaniel pup I've heard of in Compton," Hasheem said eagerly, "and my mom's finally agreed that we can have a dog. She knows how much we like Brandy."

"Then you'd better be first in line outside Mr. Hamley's office — there are bound to be lots of people who want her," Neil warned.

Just then, Neil heard a voice call his name. He turned to see Mrs. Sharpe, who told him that he was wanted in the principal's office.

"What have *you* been up to?" teased Chris.

"I hope it's not about that history test," said Neil apprehensively.

"He's probably having trouble with Dotty and wants to ask your advice," Chris suggested. Dotty was Mr. Hamley's crazy Dalmatian.

"You don't think she's having pups again, do you?" said Hasheem.

"I don't know. Better go and find out what he wants, I suppose. Will you tell Mr. Collins where I am?"

Hasheem promised that he would pass on Neil's message to their science teacher, and Neil set off slowly for the principal's office. He hadn't done anything wrong, but he couldn't help feeling a bit worried.

Mr. Hamley — Smiler, as he was known to the pupils of Meadowbank School — had left his office door wide open. Neil could see him holding a sheet of paper, tapping a pencil on his large wooden desk.

"Ah, Neil, there you are. Come in." To Neil's amazement, Smiler actually smiled! So he *hadn't* done anything wrong. Phew!

Mr. Hamley got straight to the point. Chris had been right — it *was* a dog-related subject that he wanted to discuss with Neil. "It's about this puppy," he said. "Since you're the school's dog expert, I thought you might be able to give me some advice. Look at this."

Neil looked at the sheet of paper and saw a list of names.

"All these people want to adopt the pup," continued Mr. Hamley. "There was a line of students wait-

ing to sign up right after the assembly. I can't see how Pauline Ford's ever going to choose an owner, so I had an idea which I'd like to run by you."

He paused. Neil was happy and flattered that the principal was consulting him, and curious about what he would come up with. But he wasn't the slightest bit prepared for Mr. Hamley's next words. "I thought of turning it into a competition. Everyone who's interested would have to do something, and the best entry would win the pup. What do you think?"

Neil was horrified. The thought of any animal being put up as a competition prize appalled him. It was totally irresponsible! But how in the world could he tell that to Mr. Hamley when he was looking so pleased with himself?

CHAPTER THREE

Neil was speechless. Fortunately, Mr. Hamley came to his rescue. "I can see from your expression that you don't think much of my idea, Neil."

Neil grimaced. "When we're choosing owners for dogs at King Street Kennels, we pick them on the basis of how responsible they seem," he said tactfully. "It's not enough just to *want* a dog. You've got to be completely committed to looking after it and training it."

Mr. Hamley frowned, then nodded. "Hmm. Commitment — that's the word," he said. "I think you're right, you know. But I'm still left with the same problem. How do we decide who would be the best owner for Poppy's pup?"

Inspiration suddenly came to Neil, and he grinned.

"You just said it, Mr. Hamley. *Commitment*. I think anyone who wants to adopt the pup should have to prove how committed they are to animals and their welfare."

"But how?" Mr. Hamley looked thoughtful. Then his eyes brightened behind his rectangular glasses. "What about asking everyone who's interested to present a piece of work all about their commitment to animal welfare?"

"You mean, an essay or a project?" said Neil. He liked the idea. The chances were that anyone who wasn't really determined to have a dog would drop out at this stage. Only real dog lovers would make the effort.

"A project, yes. Words, photographs, drawings — anything to show what they've done for animals over the past year. What do you think?" Mr. Hamley asked enthusiastically.

"I think it's a great idea," said Neil, grinning. It seemed like the perfect way to find the best possible home for the pup.

By the time Neil left school at the end of the afternoon, a large sheet of paper had been pinned up on the main bulletin board. It gave details of the competition, and said that anybody who was interested in adopting the puppy should hand in their project to Mr. Hamley by Friday. Hasheem and Rehana stared at it in dismay.

"*Friday*? That's impossible! It hardly gives us any time at all." Hasheem moaned.

"But that puppy would be perfect!" said Rehana, looking up at her brother. "We've *got* to do it!"

"I could draw some pictures for you," offered Sarah. Neil and Emily's little sister loved drawing and painting.

"It's not fair! Why couldn't he give us until *next* Friday?" groaned Hasheem.

"Because it's a test to see how dedicated people really are. If they really want the pup that badly, they'll drop everything else and concentrate on their project," explained Neil.

"I guess you're right," said Hasheem doubtfully.

"Are you really serious about having this puppy?" Neil asked him as the two of them walked toward the bike racks.

"You bet!" said Hasheem.

"But you haven't exactly spent a lot of time with animals, have you?" Neil commented.

Hasheem grinned. "That's what *you* think!"

"What do you mean?" Neil was intrigued.

"I've been helping out at Priorsfield Farm." Hasheem's dark eyes twinkled.

"You mean you've been going up there and helping Harry Grey? And you've never said anything to any of us? I don't believe it!" Neil laughed.

"Remember when our class went on that field trip to the farm?" said Hasheem. "Well, I made the mistake of telling Rehana all about the lambs and new-born calves and she badgered Dad into taking us there one weekend. Me and my big mouth! Next thing I knew, I was taking her there every weekend!" Hasheem grinned and looked a bit embarrassed. "We've done lots of things — cleaning out cowsheds, collecting eggs from the hens . . . One day Harry even let me drive the tractor! Hey, could you do me a favor, Neil?"

"What kind of a favor?" asked Neil.

"When I've written it, would you mind reading my essay over for me, to make sure it sounds OK?"

"No problem!" Neil agreed, impressed by his friend's enthusiasm, but a little surprised, too.

"Thanks. I'm off to get started on it now!" Hasheem jumped on his bike and rode off.

Neil followed, and had almost reached King Street Kennels when he remembered an errand that he had to run for his mom. He turned back and headed in the direction of local vet Mike Turner's clinic. He had promised to pick up some medicine for one of the rescue dogs.

On his way back from the clinic, he passed Jim Brewster's house and saw Mrs. Jepson standing on the doorstep with Sugar and Spice on rhinestone-studded leashes. The Westies' owner looked furious. The louder she shouted, the louder the two West Highland terriers yapped. Neil stopped.

"I wrote that advertisement myself and handed it

in in person," Mrs. Jepson insisted, her cheeks scarlet. "There couldn't have been any mistake!"

Jim put out a hand to restrain Skip, who was growling at Sugar and Spice and their hysterical owner. "All I'm saying is that Jake Fielding from the *Compton News* called the station today to check whether the Puppy Express trip was on Saturday or Sunday," he said wearily. "He questioned it because the ad we sent them originally said Sunday — but they also got a telephone message saying that it was on Saturday."

"It had nothing to do with *me*!" Mrs. Jepson's voice had risen to a screech. "If you're accusing me, I'll —"

"Er, excuse me, I need a quick word with Jim," said Neil quickly. He could see that the signalman needed rescuing.

"Huh! Well, I'll be off, then. I've said all I have to say," Mrs. Jepson strode toward her car, dragging the protesting Westies after her.

"Phew!" said Jim. "Thank goodness you showed up when you did. She seems to like blaming me for everything that goes wrong, and her timing couldn't be worse! I just got back from work and I'm desperate for a shower and a cup of tea."

Neil reached down to Skip, who was looking eagerly up at him, hoping for a pat. Neil rubbed the collie's ears.

"The leaflets are here. They're down at the station," Jim told him.

"Finally! Can we come and pick them up later?" asked Neil.

"Of course you can. I'll be there around half-past six. And thanks again for rescuing me from you-know-who!" Jim laughed.

"Come on, Jake, we're taking you with us to see Old Bessie," Neil told the Border collie later that evening. Jake, who had been dozing by the open kitchen door, sprang to his feet and followed Neil out into the courtyard.

Just as Neil and Emily were getting on their bikes, Sarah came running up, her dark brown braids bouncing on her shoulders.

"Look what I found!" she said happily, waving a tiny leaf at Neil and Emily.

"What is it?" Emily asked, inspecting the wilting object.

"It's a four-leaf clover. I found it in the exercise field. I'm going to give it to Rehana for good luck, so she'll get the puppy!" said Sarah.

"That's great, Squirt," Neil said. "Make sure you put it in water now, or it won't live till tomorrow."

They sped off, with Jake running alongside Neil's bike. Hasheem was waiting for them at the station when they arrived. Neil had arranged to meet him there, because he knew how much his friend would enjoy the tour of Old Bessie that Jim had promised them.

"Hello, Jake," Hasheem said, scratching behind the collie's ears and rubbing his chest. Neil noticed how well Jake responded to him, wagging his tail and nudging Hasheem's hand with his nose. Dogs seemed to like Hasheem instinctively, which was a good sign if he was ever to become a dog owner.

They found Jim and Dan Cooper, the engine driver, sitting in their workshop at the back of one of the sheds, scowling at a pile of leaflets. Even Skip looked fed up. He was lying under Jim's workbench with his head on his paws. Jake trotted up to him and nudged him with his nose, then lay down beside him.

"What's up?" asked Neil.

"The printers have messed up. The flyers say that the event starts at two o'clock instead of twelve." Jim looked as if he was about to explode with annoyance. "What *is* Mrs. Jepson up to? First, the newspaper advertising department is told the wrong day, and now the printers have got the wrong time."

"When I picked them up today, the girl at the printers told me that they'd done the 'corrections' that had been phoned in," said Dan. He was a short, wiry man of around sixty, and just now his thin face was a map of worried wrinkles.

Neil frowned. "Someone phoned in so-called corrections to the *Compton News*, and now there's been a call to the printers as well. Don't you think that's a strange coincidence?" he said.

The two men looked at one another. Then Jim said, "There have been other things, too, like things going missing. It started with the stencils I bought. I know I left them in the workshop, but they just seemed to disappear. Then two cans of engine paint vanished, and now I can't find the gold paint that arrived this morning."

"And what about the posters?" added Dan. "The printer says that he gave them to Debbie, the ticket clerk at the station, but she says that she's never seen them."

"It could just be petty theft. The station security isn't that great," said Jim, but he sounded doubtful.

"Maybe somebody's trying to sabotage the event. Someone with a grudge," Neil said thoughtfully.

"But who'd want to do that? The Puppy Express trip is for such a good cause," Emily said.

"Everyone involved in it is a dog owner, too," Jim pointed out. "And I can't think of anyone who'd want to deprive Bessie of her memorial."

"I've got an idea," said Hasheem. He turned to Neil and Emily. "Why don't we take these leaflets home and alter them by hand? We could do a third each."

"What about your project? Will you have time to do both?" Emily asked him.

Hasheem grinned. "Sure. It's going fine. Rehana and I have already done half of it."

"Great!" said Neil. "It's a deal."

Dan and Jim looked relieved.

"Since we're helping you out, d'you think we could have a look around Old Bessie's cab now?" Neil asked with a grin. He exchanged hopeful glances with Emily and Hasheem.

"Why not!" Dan laughed. "We fired her up earlier today, so she's still got plenty of steam in her boiler."

"You mean you'll take us for a ride, too?" asked Emily.

Dan nodded. Neil could hardly believe his luck. His dad would really be jealous!

"Skip, stay! We can't take you with us, I'm afraid," said Jim. The Border collie thumped his tail on the floor. Jake sprang up and ran over to Neil.

"I'd prefer not to leave Jake," he said. "He's younger than Skip and not quite as well trained. I'd be worried about him running alongside the train."

"Tell you what," Hasheem offered. "I'll stay with the dogs, if you like."

"Are you sure?" asked Neil doubtfully.

"No problem. I'll be going on the Puppy Express on Sunday — I don't mind missing out today. I'd like my guided tour of the cab, though, before you go," Hasheem said.

Dan and Jim proudly showed the three of them around the huge engine.

"She weighs nearly fifty tons," Dan said.

"And every bit of her has been restored by us, with a little help from some of the other steam train club members," said Jim.

Neil could tell how much they loved Old Bessie. She was a work of art.

"What's that for?" asked Emily, pointing to a box attached to the back of the engine.

"That's called the tender. It carries coal for the engine," explained Dan.

"How does the engine work?" asked Hasheem.

"Well, you can't just climb in and switch it on, like a car," said Jim. "Starting up an engine takes a lot of preparation. In the days when steam trains ran all over Britain, someone called a 'steam-raiser' would come and fire up the boiler in the morning. It had to be done about two hours before the engine was needed, so that the boiler got hot enough."

"How long ago was that?" asked Emily.

"Well, the very first steam train in Britain, *The Locomotion*, was built in 1825."

"Wow! Nearly two hundred years ago," exclaimed Neil.

"I still don't understand how it works, though," said Emily.

"Climb aboard and I'll show you," offered Jim.

One by one, they climbed into the cramped cab of the engine. Neil had never seen so many levers and dials. They were huge compared to the controls in a car.

"Phew, it's hot in here!" said Hasheem.

"You're standing next to the firebox," observed Jim. "That's why."

"What's that for?" asked Emily.

"You take coal from the tender, and shovel it into the firebox. The heat of the fire boils the water, which creates steam," explained Jim. "Then the steam drives pistons, which make the wheels go round."

"What does this do?" Hasheem asked, pointing to a curved brass lever.

"That's the regulator. It controls the amount of steam going to the pistons that drive the engine, so it can make the train slow down or speed up." He pushed the lever up and down to demonstrate.

"Like a kind of brake?" asked Neil.

"No, because it can't stop the train completely. This is the brake here." Dan pointed to a lever on his left. "To stop the train, you have to use both the regulator and the brake," he explained.

"I see," said Neil, but he didn't really, and Dan could tell from his expression.

"Watch what I do when we take her out," he said. "Then you'll get a better idea of how it all works."

"I'd better get off," said Hasheem. "Enjoy your trip!"

"We're only going a couple of hundred yards down the line." Dan laughed.

"Where's Jake?" asked Neil.

Hearing Neil's voice, the collie ran out of the bushes. He stood next to Hasheem and barked at Neil.

"It's OK, boy. Stay there! Here's his leash. Catch!" Neil took the leash out of his pocket and threw it to Hasheem, who clipped it onto Jake's collar.

Dan pulled a lever. There was a hiss of steam, a squeal from the wheels, and they were off, puffing out of Compton Station along the recently renovated track. Hasheem stood on the platform, waving them off. Neil could see Jake and Skip, but couldn't hear their barks over the din of the engine.

Just beyond Compton Station, Dan slowed the train down and let Neil blow the whistle. The driver pulled the lever to put the engine into reverse and they puffed backward on the tracks.

On Sunday, Bessie's coaches would be attached —

full of dogs and their owners, all happily enjoying the ride. It was going to be great, Neil thought. But as the engine hissed to a stop, he began to have doubts. What if something else went wrong before Sunday? After all the mysterious happenings, Neil was convinced that something very strange was going on. He was determined to find out exactly what it was. . . .

CHAPTER FOUR

In assembly on Friday, Mr. Hamley announced that he had received five projects. He said he would take them home so that he and Pauline Ford could read them over the weekend.

"On Monday, I'll announce the name of the person who we think would be the most suitable owner for this puppy," said the principal. "They can then come along and meet the pup. If by any chance they decide that it's not the right one for them, then I'll contact the person who gave in the second-best project. That seems the fairest way to decide the matter."

Five projects . . . and Rusty has four pups, thought Neil. Perhaps he could persuade the people who couldn't have the spaniel to come over to the rescue center and meet Rusty's pups. And Rusty needed a home, too. She was a gentle, well-trained dog who would make someone a wonderful pet.

As Mr. Hamley went on about more dates for cricket and netball matches, Neil glanced at Hasheem. His face was expressionless, but his eyes gave him away. Neil knew he wanted the springer spaniel pup very badly.

"We're going to raise *tons* of money for Bessie's memorial," Emily said as she and Neil helped the kennel assistants, Bev and Kate, feed the boarding dogs the next morning. "We've sold tickets to so many people," she continued. "Bev, who'll bring Milly, the Thomsons and Digger, Mr. and Mrs. Harding with Jessie . . ."

"I sold a ticket to Mr. Hamley, too. He and Dotty are boarding the train at Padsham," Neil told Emily. "By the way, speaking of Padsham, isn't there an art shop there? Jim still can't find his gold paint, so I thought we could get some more for him."

"OK. Let's go and have a look later. There's Mike!" Emily waved to the vet, who had just arrived for his regular Saturday morning dog clinic.

"Do you need a hand?" Neil asked him.

"Yes, please," said Mike.

Neil and Emily went to help him unload boxes and bags from the trunk of his car.

Mike glanced up at the sky and made a face. "It looks like rain," he said.

"I hope it's clear for the trip tomorrow," said Emily.

The vet unlocked the door of the old rescue center, where he ran his clinic, and held it open so that Neil could get past with the box of leaflets on dog care. Neil was just coming back out when he heard a call from Emily.

"Oh, no! It's Mrs. Jepson!"

The white Volvo crawled through the main gates at such a slow pace that Neil wondered if there was something wrong with it. But when Mrs. Jepson got out, he realized what the matter was. In her arms, she held a blanket-wrapped form of a small West Highland terrier. Her thick coat of makeup was smudged from crying.

"Is it Sugar or Spice?" Neil asked anxiously, staring at the small, shivering bundle.

"It's Sugar," Mrs. Jepson replied in a hoarse voice.

"What happened?" said Neil.

"I think somebody poisoned her," Mrs. Jepson sobbed. "I need to see Mike immediately."

"Let's take her straight in," Neil said briskly.

Sugar seemed weak and listless as the vet gently placed her on the examination table. "How long has she been like this?" he asked, concerned.

"Since late yesterday evening," replied Mrs. Jepson. "I thought she'd just gobbled her food too fast — you know how greedy she is. But she just went on being sick and there was foam around her mouth. She was sneezing a lot, too."

Mike frowned. "Let's have a look in your mouth, little one," he said to Sugar. Neil and Emily watched as he placed his hand on her whiskery muzzle. Sugar gave a little whimper.

"It's all right, Sugar," Mrs. Jepson said soothingly, stroking the terrier's trembling back.

Mike suddenly stared at his fingers. "There's some kind of white powder on her," he said. "Have you been dry-shampooing her, or putting talcum powder on her fur?"

Mrs. Jepson shook her head.

Mike put his face close to Sugar and sniffed her

fur. "She smells of perfume, too," he said. He took another sniff. "It smells just like laundry detergent."

"It can't be laundry detergent," insisted Mrs. Jepson. "I keep that in a cupboard in the utility room. Sugar and Spice were in the kitchen most of the evening. My husband and I were in the sitting room with the rest of the steam train committee, sorting out the final details for tomorrow. There's no way the dogs could have eaten anything other than the food I put down for them."

"And Spice is all right?"

"Yes," Mrs. Jepson assured Mike.

Mike took Sugar's temperature and continued to examine her, peering down her throat and gently feeling her abdomen. Eventually, he looked up. "I don't think she's in any grave danger," he said. "But she's really dehydrated. I think we should put her on a drip right away and get some fluids into her. The more liquid she gets into her system, the faster she'll flush out anything that could be disagreeing with her," he explained.

"Oh, my poor darling!" sobbed Mrs. Jepson.

Mike glanced out the door, where a line of people and their dogs was building up. "I need to take her down to my clinic right now. Neil, could you explain, and tell everyone that I'll be back as soon as I can?"

"No problem," said Neil.

Mike got a pair of scissors out of his bag and snipped off a small piece of fur from beneath Sugar's chin.

"What are you doing?" Mrs. Jepson asked, horrified. "I want Sugar to look her best for tomorrow. She *will* be OK for tomorrow, won't she?"

Neil and Emily exchanged glances. Neil could tell that Emily was as horrified as he was. Surely even Mrs. Jepson wouldn't put her own moment of fame before the health of her dog?

"I think you'd better face the fact that this little dog might not be well enough to undertake her public duties tomorrow, Mrs. Jepson," Mike said firmly. "Spice will just have to do it by himself. I need to send a clipping of Sugar's fur to the lab for analysis, to find out what that powder is. I won't get the results until this evening at the earliest, so in the meantime, let's concentrate on getting Sugar better."

Mike settled the Westie into a dog carrier and drove off to his clinic in the center of Compton. Mrs. Jepson followed close behind in her car. Neil was left to explain to a line of very understanding people that Sugar's case was an emergency and that Mike would be coming back as soon as he could.

"Hey, Em, d'you mind staying here for a bit?" asked Neil. "I haven't had a chance to check up on Rusty's pups yet."

"Sure," said Emily.

Neil found Kate crouched by Rusty's pen with the smallest puppy cradled in her hand. The puppy was sucking at the tip of a plastic bottle that Kate held up for her. Once Neil had discovered her brothers weren't letting her get any milk, Kate and Carole had been taking turns feeding her by bottle.

"How's she doing?" asked Neil softly.

"She's still very weak," said Kate. "Do you want to take a turn?"

Neil gently took the puppy and the bottle, and continued with the feeding. He told Kate about Sugar. "Do you think Sugar'll be OK?" he asked her.

"It depends on what she's eaten," said Kate. "Mrs. Jepson should have called Mike yesterday evening when Sugar first got sick. It may not be a poisonous substance at all. Sugar could have swallowed something that caused an obstruction in her stomach, or she could even have a virus of some sort."

"But she had white powder around her mouth," said Neil. "And don't you think it's odd that Sugar's ill while Spice is all right? If it was something in their food, surely they'd *both* be sick."

"Hmm. It does seem strange," replied Kate. "Let's just hope that Mike doesn't find anything too serious . . ."

When Neil went back to the old rescue center, a few drops of rain had begun to fall. He decided to keep Mike's customers entertained by giving out the vet's latest batch of leaflets about dog care during the summer months. As soon as Mike returned, Neil asked him about Sugar.

"There was a visible improvement as soon as we put her on the drip," Mike said. "She stopped being sick and went to sleep. I estimate that by this evening she'll be able to go home." He smiled at Neil and Emily's obvious relief, and welcomed in his first patient.

"Tell you what, Em. It's cooler now that it's started to rain. How about we bike over to Padsham and look for that paint for Jim?"

"Good idea," said Emily.

With Jake bounding along beside them, they set off for Padsham. The rain wasn't heavy, and it was quite refreshing to feel it on their hands and faces after the last few days of hot weather. They found the art shop, bought the gold paint, then headed straight for Compton Station.

As soon as they turned down the path to the engine sheds, Jake started barking. Neil looked at Emily and grinned. "That means Skip and Jim must be —" he began. But before he could finish, Skip came rushing out of a shed, and he and Jake rolled over playfully, happy to see each other.

They found Jim sawing some wood on his workbench. "I'm just repairing a split panel in one of the coaches," he explained.

Dan had a wrench in his hand and was tightening the nuts on one of the wheels. "In the old days, they used to check the nuts and bolts on every single coach and engine every day," he said.

Emily handed over two small cans of paint. "That

was all we could afford," she said. "I hope it's going to be enough."

"As long as I've got enough to paint Old Bessie's name, nothing else really matters," Jim said cheerfully. "We can do the rest of the gilding another time. Thanks for getting it! Now how much do I owe you?"

Neil handed him the receipt and he delved in his pocket and counted out the money.

"We've made a lot of progress since Mrs. Jepson stopped checking up on us," said Dan. "We haven't seen her since yesterday afternoon."

Neil glanced at Emily. "There's a reason for that. Sugar's ill," he explained.

"Yes. Mrs. Jepson thinks she ate something poisonous," added Emily.

Both men looked concerned.

"She's getting better now, though," Emily assured them.

"I'm glad to hear it," said Jim. "Sugar and Spice may be little terrors, but nobody likes to hear of a dog being sick. I've been lucky with Skip. He's never had a day's illness, have you, boy?"

The collie nudged Jim with his cold, wet nose, and his owner ruffled his fur. Jake immediately demanded the same treatment from Neil.

"By the way," Neil said as he rubbed one of Jake's silky black ears, "we saw the poster outside the station. It looks great!" It had the words *Puppy Express* in big letters at the top, and details of the steam train trip at the bottom. In the center, there was a reproduction of a photo of Bessie the golden retriever, from Mrs. Maitland-Smith's family album.

"My nephew designed it. He's an art student," said Dan proudly.

"I see the council got their act together and put up signs directing people to the station, too," said Neil.

"We altered all those flyers like we promised," added Emily. "We've given lots out at school."

"And we're going to give out the rest and try to sell more tickets at the supermarket this afternoon," promised Neil.

"Thanks a lot," said Jim gratefully. "With your help, it looks like Old Bessie's maiden journey will be a great success, after all."

But Neil and Emily discovered yet another setback later that day.

After dinner, exhausted but satisfied with their day's work, they collapsed on the couch to watch the end of the local news while they waited for their favorite nature program to start. Neil wasn't really listening. He was working knots and burs out of Jake's tail with a dog comb.

Suddenly, Emily gave a start. "Oh, no!" she cried, jumping up. "Neil, look!"

Neil glanced at the screen and saw someone being interviewed at Manchester Airport. It took him a couple of seconds to realize who it was. The young man who had been accosted by the news reporter as he headed off for a vacation in the Seychelles was none other than the famous soccer player Marcus Welham. But what was he doing leaving the country when he was supposed to be at Compton Station the next day, cutting the ribbon and declaring the Puppy Express event open?

CHAPTER FIVE

"**W**hy would Marcus let us down?" cried Emily in dismay.

"Hang on. Let me think . . ." Neil's mind was racing. What could have gone wrong? According to Mrs. Jepson, Marcus had been booked weeks ago to open the event.

Bob Parker walked into the room and saw their troubled faces. "Mrs. Jepson couldn't organize a food fight in a supermarket!" he said in exasperation when Neil told him what had happened. "They should have let Mrs. Maitland-Smith sort things out. Look how well she runs the stables and that big house of hers. She'd be a brilliant manager."

"Well, she's not organizing it, unfortunately," said

Emily. "So what are we going to do about tomorrow? Everyone was really looking forward to seeing Marcus — and Amber."

"This is really weird," said Neil. "I can't help thinking that someone's trying to sabotage the event."

"It's more likely that Mrs. Jepson told Marcus the wrong date," said Bob. "She's managed to mix everything else up."

"Let's call her now, in case she didn't see the local news," Emily suggested sensibly.

Neil and Emily went to the phone in the hall and Neil dialed Mrs. Jepson's number. When he told her about Marcus, she was horrified.

"But he *promised*!" she wailed. "Oh, dear. As if it wasn't enough with poor Sugar being ill . . . I'm just about to get her from Mike's clinic now."

"I'm glad she's better, but we've still got to sort out this problem before tomorrow," Neil said urgently. "We need someone else to launch the event."

"Oh, dear," said Mrs. Jepson again. She sounded as if she was in a complete panic. "How in the world are we going to find a celebrity who's free at such short notice?" She paused, then said, "This should be Mrs. Maitland-Smith's responsibility. She's the one who knows Marcus and who made the arrangement with him. Let *her* sort out the problem! Would you do me a favor and call her for me, Neil? I really can't stand the woman. Now, I must run and fetch my darling Sugar."

Neil heard the loud crash as she banged the receiver down.

"Huh! Talk about passing the buck!" he snorted.

"What do you mean?" asked Emily.

Neil explained. "She might be right, though," he added. "It probably *is* Mrs. Maitland-Smith's job to find a replacement. Let's call her now."

Neil found her number in the phone book, but there was no reply and no answering machine, either. "This is serious," he said solemnly. "We can't wait for her — she could be out for hours."

"How about Mr. Hamley? He could open the event. Or how about Dad? Everyone knows him *and* he's connected with dogs!" suggested Emily.

"What, *me*?" Bob called from the sitting room. He gave a loud laugh. "I'm hardly a famous personality, am I?"

Neil walked back into the room. "Well, it should be someone connected with dogs, since most of the money is going toward Bessie's memorial," he said.

"What about Sergeant Moorhead? Everybody knows him and Sherlock," said Emily eagerly. Sherlock was Compton's own police dog, a talented and lovable German shepherd.

"You know, that's not a bad idea, Em," agreed Neil. "What do you think, Dad?"

"Great," said Bob. "I'm sure he'd be very flattered."

But there was no reply at Sergeant Moorhead's number, either, so Neil left a message on his answering machine, saying that it was urgent and asking the sergeant to call back.

"Don't get your hopes up, Neil. He could be on duty tomorrow," Bob warned.

Having tried Mrs. Maitland-Smith's number again with no success, Neil suggested that they go to her house to slip a message under the door.

"Good idea," said Emily. "And she might not be out, you know — she could be in the stables, or somewhere on the grounds of her house. Let's go!"

Half an hour later, Neil and Emily reached the big white gates that led to the driveway of Honeybourne House. Jake squeezed through the wooden bars, but Neil and Emily had to open the gate and wheel their bikes through. The stables were beside the house, and there were some beautiful horses grazing in a field. As they approached, Jake suddenly thrust his muzzle into the air, sniffed, then barked loudly. He was answered by a flurry of high-pitched barks, and Jemima came rushing out of the stable yard. She stood on her hind legs and pranced around Jake. Her black, woolly pom-poms looked ridiculous next to Jake's sleek, natural coat.

"She looks like a bush that they've done topi . . . topi-thingy on," said Emily. "You know, those fancy-shaped bushes?"

"You mean topiary." Neil laughed. "Yes, she does. Here, girl." He took a dog treat out of his pocket. The

poodle took it gently. *She's obviously very well
trained*, thought Neil admiringly. If Mrs. Maitland-
Smith had trained Jemima herself, she had done a
good job. Pity she was so haughty, though. It made
her a bit difficult to like, even if she was a dog lover.
He gave Jake a treat, too, then he and Emily headed
for the stables.

Emily was right about finding Mrs. Maitland-
Smith there. She was holding the bridle of a beauti-
ful black thoroughbred while a groom removed the
mare's saddle. She looked surprised to see Neil and
Emily — and was horrified when they told her about
Marcus.

"But he *knew* it was tomorrow. How dare he go on
vacation?" she said. "Once these stars get a bit of

fame and money, it just goes to their heads. They get selfish and can't think of anyone but themselves."

"I don't think Marcus is like that!" said Neil. "He's always seemed really friendly and down-to-earth when I've met him. I'm sure he wouldn't let down a good cause like this one — especially since he thinks the world of his own dog."

"Nice guy or not, he obviously preferred the Seychelles to Compton Station," Mrs. Maitland-Smith said cynically.

There was no point in arguing with her, Neil decided. This was an emergency that needed to be straightened out right away.

"We thought of asking Sergeant Moorhead to open the event instead, but he's not in," he explained.

"Anyway, he might be on duty tomorrow," added Emily. "Can you think of anyone else who'd be free on such short notice?"

Mrs. Maitland-Smith frowned. "I *can* think of someone," she said slowly. "Someone who's not only free, but who would also be very suitable indeed."

"Who's that?" asked Emily.

"If Sergeant Moorhead isn't free, then I can promise you that the person I have in mind will definitely do it. Just call me before the end of the evening and tell me if you've heard from him," Mrs. Maitland-Smith said. "Now, would you like to look around the stables?" she asked, quickly changing the subject. "Jake's all right with horses, isn't he?"

"Of course he is. He's been well trained . . . so has Jemima, hasn't she?"

Neil, Emily, and Mrs. Maitland-Smith talked dogs and horses for the next half an hour, and Neil found himself warming to Jemima's owner. She might be a bit snooty with people, but with animals she was a different person. Her horses obviously respected and obeyed her, and she rewarded them with strokes and pats and words of praise. Neil approved.

"Who do you think she meant? Maybe someone famous rides at her stables. An actress or something," Emily said as they biked back to King Street.

"I think she might have said something if it was someone really famous," Neil replied. "Let's just wait and see."

When they got home, Sergeant Moorhead hadn't called — and Neil was almost sure he wasn't going to. It looked like their plans for the Puppy Express were going off the rails.

Emily distracted herself with some geography homework, but Neil was restless and couldn't concentrate on anything, so he went out to the kennel. Jake jumped up from his favorite spot by the back door and padded after him. It was eight o'clock, and the sun was setting behind the trees on the hill, and spreading long fingers of shadow across the courtyard. A few dogs yapped as they heard Neil's footsteps. He peered in every cage and greeted every boarder, then went over to the rescue center. In addition to Rusty and her pups, there were three other residents — a mournful-looking boxer, a lively terrier badly in need of training, and a tan mongrel with a skin problem that Mike was treating.

Neil petted the dogs and gave each a treat, then turned his attention to Rusty. Three fat pups were nursing greedily, but once again the smallest one had gotten sidelined and was crouching by her mother's tail, whimpering.

"Come here, little one," said Neil. He reached in and scooped the puppy up. The little warm body squirmed in his hand. Neil could still feel the pup's bones where there should have been a padding of puppy fat. Neil decided she could use another bottle feed, and went to find his mother.

Carole was in the office, working late on some paperwork. "Hello, Neil. I sometimes think I should employ a secretary," she grumbled. "Who've you got there?"

"It's Rusty's smallest pup," said Neil. "I think she could use some more milk."

"Yes, I haven't gotten around to it yet, poor little thing. I'll mix the formula, if you'd like to do the feeding," said Carole.

While Neil held the pup and murmured soothingly to her, his mother warmed a feeding bottle. When it had reached the right temperature, she handed it to Neil. He placed the bottle by the puppy's mouth. She sniffed it, realized that it held something delicious, and began to suck thirstily. Neil smiled as he watched her. There were few sights better than small pups feeding.

"She's quite a greedy little thing, given a chance. She'll be fine before long," said Carole. "It might be a good idea to keep an eye on her weight for a few days, though."

They both stroked and admired the ginger-colored pup.

"She's so lovely. There's no way we'll have trouble finding homes for the litter," said Neil. "And for Rusty, too, I hope. I just wish that Mr. Hamley —"

Carole cut him off. "I'm sorry. Neil, but he can't advertise *every* rescue puppy for us — it's not his job. Mrs. Ford's springer spaniel pup was an exception."

"We'll find out who's getting her on Monday. I hope it's Hasheem and Rehana," Neil said.

Carole took the puppy back to the rescue center and placed her gently back with her mother. "Your dad told me about Marcus Welham letting everyone down," she said to Neil. "I think Sergeant Moorhead might be on vacation, though. I'm sure he mentioned that he was going to go hiking in the Lake District in the middle of June — if he could get the time off."

"Mrs. Maitland-Smith said she knew someone else who could do it, if Sergeant Moorhead couldn't," Neil told her.

"I hope she does. I don't think Mrs. Jepson will be able to cope otherwise," said Carole.

By ten o'clock that evening there had been no word from Sergeant Moorhead.

"I think I'd better call Mrs. Maitland-Smith and tell her, so that she can book this mystery person," Neil said, yawning. "I hope it's somebody who knows all about the story of Bessie, 'cause they've got to give an opening speech."

Neil dialed Mrs. Maitland-Smith's number. She picked the receiver up right away, as if she'd been expecting his call, and Neil quickly told her the news.

"So I guess we're relying on this person you said you knew," he finished. "Who is it? Are they famous?"

"She's not famous exactly, but lots of people know her," Mrs. Maitland-Smith replied.

Who could it be? Neil wondered. An actress? A sports personality? He had no idea what kind of people Mrs. Maitland-Smith knew. Maybe it was a famous show jumper . . .

"Are you sure she'll do a good job?" he asked anxiously. "After all, she won't have long to prepare a speech."

"She doesn't need to prepare a speech — she knows all about Bessie already," Mrs. Maitland-Smith assured him briskly.

"Who *is* it then?" he asked, bursting with curiosity.

"Me!" she replied at last.

CHAPTER SIX

"**Y**ou?" Neil exclaimed, realizing too late that he might have sounded a bit rude.

"Why not, Neil?" Mrs. Maitland-Smith sounded amused. "Bessie was my grandmother's dog. The purpose of the event is to raise money for Bessie's memorial and to pay the costs of restoring the engine that was named after her. So who better to open the event than me? I'm well known in the area — lots of local people come here for riding lessons. I may not be a superstar like Marcus Welham, but I think I'll do a good job. I'll call Mrs. Jepson right now and tell her."

Neil wasn't sure what to think. He said good-bye and walked back into the living room to tell everyone.

"Well, I think she's right about being the best person for the job," declared Bob. "It'll make a good story for the press, having the granddaughter of Bessie's owner launch the Puppy Express ride."

"I guess so," said Neil, still feeling uncertain.

"So, everything's settled then," said Bob. "It should be a great day tomorrow."

"I wonder how Sugar is now?" Neil said.

"Why don't you call Mrs. Jepson to find out? Wait ten minutes or so, though. She and Mrs. Maitland-Smith are probably in the middle of a shouting match!" Bob laughed. Then he added, "Actually, they may sort out their differences, now that Mrs. Maitland-Smith has a proper role to play. I'm not surprised that she was a bit miffed when Mrs. Jepson was made chairperson."

"It is a bit unfair," Neil agreed. He waited a while, then dialed Mrs. Jepson's number. Mr. Jepson picked up the phone at the other end. Neil could hear his wife calling to him. "If it's Mrs. Maitland-Smith again, I've gone out!" His dad had obviously been wrong about the two women settling their differences!

"Oh, Neil, that *woman*!" Mrs. Jepson complained when she eventually took the call. "All those airs and graces! But I suppose I should be glad that she's jumped in to save the day for us. Pity she couldn't have found a TV star or someone, though."

"How's Sugar?" asked Neil, changing the subject.

"She's back from Mike's and she's much better,

thanks," Mrs. Jepson said. "And guess what? Mike got the results of the analysis and it *was* laundry detergent on her fur. I can't figure out where it came from. I'm pretty sure she'll be OK for tomorrow, though. We can't have her missing her starring role, can we, Spice?"

Neil heard a combination of scratching and slurping noises.

"Stop it, Spice! He's trying to eat the phone," Mrs. Jepson told Neil. "You naughty boy . . . I'll just put him down. He's jealous of all the attention I'm giving Sugar. Now, I must go. I've got to get my babies shampooed and combed, ready for tomorrow."

"Did Mike say it was all right to take Sugar?" Neil asked anxiously.

"Neil! You don't think I'd risk her health, do you?" scolded Mrs. Jepson.

Neil sighed quietly. "No, of course I don't," he said, trying to convince himself that he meant it.

"I wish I was coming with you," said Carole as she waved them off the next morning. "But someone's got to stay to keep an eye on things. We've got four people coming to pick up their dogs today."

"And I'm going to Kayleigh's birthday party!" announced Sarah. "It's a costume party and I'm going to be a fairy."

"I wouldn't be surprised if Mrs. Jepson was in costume today," said Carole, raising an eyebrow.

Neil and Emily caught each other's eye and burst
out laughing at the thought.

Their mom was not far off the mark. Mrs. Jepson
was dressed in a long blue satin dress with matching
blue bows in her blond curls. She carried a straw
basket decorated with blue and pink ribbons, and
peeping out of it were two mischievous white
faces — Sugar and Spice, each wearing a bow. Neil
found it hard not to laugh when Emily nudged him.

They had arrived at Compton Station just before

half-past ten to find a line of excited people already there, waiting to buy tickets. The sun was hot, but Mr. Jepson and a couple of helpers were standing behind a table in a shady spot, selling tickets.

"Oh, good!" said the councilor. "I'm glad you two have arrived. Perhaps you can take over my job so that I can get on with a few other things."

"Sure," said Emily.

They took off their backpacks, which were heavy with bottles of water to keep themselves and Jake hydrated throughout the day, and stood behind the ticket desk.

"Hello, Mrs. Hammond," Emily said, greeting their neighbor. When Jake saw his mother, Delilah, he trotted up and sniffed noses with her. Delilah licked Jake's face.

By half-past-eleven, when the event was due to begin, the station was packed with people and their dogs. Through the open doors, Old Bessie could be seen waiting by the platform with steam coming from her funnel.

"I think I'd better put Jake on the leash now," said Neil. "Mrs. Jepson's going to announce that all dogs must be kept on leashes, so I think we should set a good example."

"Look! I can see Bev and Milly," said Emily, giving them a wave.

"Hi, Hasheem! Hi, Rehana!" called Neil as he spotted them in the crowd. The Lindons were among the few people without a dog. Neil hoped they would have one soon.

There were so many familiar faces, both human and canine, that Neil hardly knew who to greet first. There must have been at least thirty dogs present — all fairly well-behaved, apart from the odd burst of barking and leash-tugging. So far that morning, Neil had been really impressed with Jake's behavior. For a young dog, he was remarkably obedient and quick to learn. He greeted other dogs politely, sniffing them and wagging his tail in a friendly fashion. Neil rewarded him with pats and an occasional dog treat.

A camera team from the local television station was on the scene and Neil waved to Jake Fielding, the ponytailed reporter from the *Compton News*. From the conversations he overheard, Neil realized that some people had come especially to see Marcus Welham. He knew how disappointed they'd be when he didn't show up. Mrs. Jepson was going to have an awkward job explaining what had happened.

At eleven-thirty on the dot, Mrs. Jepson placed the basket containing a very restless Sugar and Spice on the floor next to her husband, climbed onto the makeshift stage outside the station, and coughed into a microphone. It whistled loudly, causing a flurry of yapping and barking. Mrs. Jepson looked around anxiously. A young man ran up, muttered something to her, then ran back and started twiddling knobs on an amplifier.

"Oh, dear," said Emily. "Poor Mrs. Jepson."

"Ahem!" Mrs. Jepson started again, holding the microphone so far from her mouth that it was almost impossible to hear her.

"Can't hear you!" bellowed a man from the back of the crowd. Mrs. Jepson looked really flustered now. The young man ran back and showed her exactly where to hold the microphone, and she finally began.

"I'm pleased to see so many people here today for this glorious event," she said. But before she could get another word out, there was an outbreak of hysterical yapping. Sugar and Spice charged toward their owner and proceeded to run around her legs, wrapping her up in their leashes. Mrs. Jepson staggered and would have fallen if her husband hadn't run up to help her.

Neil started to feel sorry for her. After all, she was trying to do her best, and everything seemed to be going against her. "At least Sugar's her usual self again," he whispered to Emily.

With the two naughty West Highland terriers firmly in Mr. Jepson's grip, the councillor's wife began her introduction again and managed to get through it this time. At the end, she introduced Mrs. Maitland-Smith with a frosty smile.

The riding-school owner slid smoothly to the microphone, with Jemima by her side.

"I'm pleased and proud to see you all here today — and especially pleased that so many of you have

brought your dogs with you," she said. "As you know, we're all here to celebrate the life of Bessie, a very special golden retriever who belonged to my grandmother. Bessie was born in 1937, and if it hadn't been for her, I wouldn't be talking to you today . . ."

She spoke like a professional, giving a dramatic account of the events of that night in Manchester long ago. Everyone held their breath as they were asked to picture the bombers roaring in the sky overhead and Bessie doing her best to wake the family and get them to safety.

"I'm proud to announce that, thanks to all of you,

we've raised all the funds we need to put up a memorial statue to Bessie, the most famous dog in Compton's history."

Everyone clapped, but Mrs. Maitland-Smith held up her hand for silence.

"I would like to thank Mr. Jepson and the Compton Council for making this event possible. I would also like to thank Jim Brewster for coming up with the idea for the memorial, and for naming the steam engine after my grandmother's dog."

She didn't thank Mrs. Jepson. Neil looked at the councilor's wife and saw her scowling.

Mrs. Maitland-Smith cut the red ribbon draped around the engine and doused Old Bessie in champagne. Everybody cheered, and Mrs. Jepson took the stage again, with Sugar and Spice snuggled in her arms.

"Those poor dogs look like stuffed toys," Emily whispered with a grin.

"All aboard the Puppy Express!" shouted Mrs. Jepson.

There was a scramble to be the first on board. Emily went ahead with her best friend Julie Baker, who was with her mother and Ben, their beautiful Old English sheepdog. Ben was looking his very best, with his shaggy coat perfectly combed and his bright brown eyes blinking through long bangs.

"Save me a seat, will you?" said Neil. "I want to give Jake some water before the trip starts." When

Jake had finished his drink, Neil climbed into the coach and walked down the aisle until he reached the table where the Parkers and the Bakers had found seats together. Jake seemed happy to see Ben again. He licked his nose, got a mouthful of Ben's hair, and sneezed.

"Silly mutt!" Neil laughed, rubbing Jake affectionately between the ears.

"That dog's the mirror image of Skip," said Emily, pointing to the Border collie who sat at the feet of a young couple at the end of the coach.

"It *is* Skip." Neil called his name and the collie turned around enquiringly. "I think those people are Jim's neighbors. I'm glad Skip's not missing out on the ride."

Soon, everybody had settled into their seats. Neil could hear voices saying, "Sit" and "Stay" as people persuaded their excited dogs to keep still. Puffs of white steam from the engine drifted past the windows. It was hot in the coach, and Neil and Emily took long swigs from their water bottles. Dogs were panting and their owners were chatting, anxious to be off.

"We should have left by now, right Dad?" Emily complained after a while. There was still no sign of the train starting to move.

Bob Parker glanced at his watch. "Yes. We're about ten minutes late. I wonder what's holding us up?"

"I'm going to find out. Em, hold Jake a minute,

OK?" Neil thrust the Border collie's leash into his sister's hand. Before Bob could stop him, he jumped off the train and ran along the platform.

Mrs. Jepson and Jim Brewster were standing by the steaming, hissing engine, which had *Puppy Express* banners draped along its sides. Sugar and Spice were barking frantically at the noisy locomotive but, for once, Mrs. Jepson was ignoring them.

"What's wrong? Why aren't we moving?" asked Neil.

"We've got no driver. Dan Cooper hasn't shown up," said Jim anxiously.

Mrs. Jepson turned to Neil. She looked as if she was on the verge of tears. "The whole day's going to be ruined!" she wailed. "We'll have to give everyone their money back. Oh, Neil, what are we going to *do*?"

CHAPTER SEVEN

Neil just couldn't believe that Dan Cooper would let them down. He'd seemed so excited about the whole event. Something must have happened to him.

"Have you seen him at all this morning?" he asked Jim.

"Yes. I gave him a wake-up call at six-thirty, and we came to the station together to start Bessie's boiler," said Jim. "We coupled the coaches on, then he went off to grab a bite to eat. He said he'd be back at ten, but I haven't seen him since. I wasn't too worried at first — I was sure he was around somewhere, chatting with people or being photographed for the paper."

"So where exactly was he last seen?" asked Neil. He had hoped that the Puppy Express's problems were over, but now he was beginning to have doubts. Perhaps someone *was* trying to sabotage the event — and perhaps they had something to do with Dan's disappearance?

"Colin saw him on Dale End Road, biking toward the station," said Jim. Colin Jones was another member of the steam train club, who was acting as guard for the event. Even now, he was parading up and down the platform with his whistle and flag, glancing anxiously at his watch.

"What time was that?" asked Neil.

"About quarter-past nine," said Jim.

"But it's only ten minutes from there to the station," said Mrs. Jepson. "Where *could* he have gone?"

"I hope he didn't have an accident," Neil said, frowning. "Has he got a cell phone?"

Jim laughed and shook his head. "I've got one, but Dan likes doing everything the old-fashioned way. He doesn't go for new technology. That's one of the reasons he loves steam engines so much."

"Is anybody else qualified to drive Old Bessie?" Neil asked Jim.

"Actually, I am. But I can't drive *and* stoke the boiler at the same time," Jim pointed out.

"I could do it!" Neil suggested hopefully.

Jim laughed and shook his head. "You're not big enough to lift that heavy shovel. It needs somebody with lots of muscle."

"Dad!" Neil said instantly. His father was big and

broad and very fit, and he loved trains. It would be the perfect solution. "What do you think?" he said to Jim.

"Well, he'd get his clothes dirty . . ." Jim warned.

"Oh, Dad won't mind that! I'm sure he'd love to do it. I'll go and ask him. But there's one more thing . . ." Neil grinned hopefully. "If Dad's the fireman, can I ride in the cab with you?"

"Oh, all right!" agreed Jim with a chuckle.

Neil raced off to tell his dad the news. As he had predicted, Bob jumped at the chance to be one of Old Bessie's crew. "I've wanted to travel in the cab of a steam train ever since I was little," he said eagerly.

Neil picked up his backpack. "Look after Jake for me, please, Em?" he said. "I hate leaving him behind, but it would be too dangerous for him in the cab. Do you mind being left on your own?"

"I'm hardly on my own!" she assured him. Neil looked up and down the coach and saw what she meant. Every seat on the clean, freshly painted coach was taken — dogs of all shapes, sizes, and breeds were poking eager faces from underneath tables, or sprawled with their forepaws or tails sticking out into the aisles. "I think Jake's quite happy, too," added Emily. "Just look at him!" Jake was stretched out on the floor next to Ben, with his head resting on one of the Old English sheepdog's huge front paws. When he saw Neil looking at him, he gave a whimper that turned into a noisy yawn.

Neil and Bob left the carriage and made their way to the driver's cab. Jim and Mrs. Jepson looked relieved to see them — and so did Sugar and Spice. They were overexcited, and started to yap wildly and tug on their leashes. But one word of command from Bob and they stopped. Mrs. Jepson looked stunned.

"Climb aboard and I'll show you what to do," Jim told Bob. As Bob took a step toward the cab, Sugar darted forward, wrapping her leash around Bob's ankles.

"Keep hold of that dog!" Bob told Mrs. Jepson sternly. "Better still, take them into one of the coaches. We'll be off in a minute — you'd better get on board now if you don't want to be left behind."

As Mrs. Jepson pulled Sugar toward her, Spice cocked his leg up against one of Old Bessie's newly gilded wheels.

"Stop that!" yelled Jim.

"Oh, dear," said Mrs. Jepson feebly, but she made no move to follow Bob's advice.

"Before we leave, don't you think we should have one last go at finding Dan?" Bob suggested, unclipping his cell phone from the waistband of his jeans. "I'll call his home, just in case there's some news."

There was no reply at Dan's house. Bob called the hospital next, but there hadn't been any accidents involving bicycles in the Compton area. It was as if Dan had vanished.

"Very mysterious," Bob said with a shrug.

"It's more than mysterious, Dad," said Neil grimly. "Don't you think Dan's 'disappearance' might have been arranged deliberately, to make sure the train couldn't go?"

"But who would want to do that?" asked Bob, looking puzzled.

Neil shrugged. "I can't think of anyone. But someone's got to be working against the Puppy Express trip. Too many things have gone wrong for them to be coincidences."

"Come on, let's get going," said Mrs. Jepson before Bob had a chance to respond. "I'll tell everyone we're about to leave, OK?"

"Go ahead," confirmed Jim.

Bob handed his cell phone to Neil. "Could you put this in your backpack? I don't want to drop it into the firebox! Now, how much coal do I put in, Jim? And how often?"

"Just put a shovelful in whenever I tell you," instructed Jim. "You don't have to heap it on all the time. The steam gauges in the cab will let me know when we need more. I'll show you in a minute. Go on, Neil, you get in first."

Neil was about to climb up into the cab when Mrs. Jepson bustled back. "The doors are all closed and everybody's ready to start," she said brightly. Sweeping in front of Neil, she scooped up Sugar, then Spice, and deposited each dog in the cab before heaving herself up after them.

"What do you think you're doing?" Jim demanded angrily. "Take those dogs out of my cab this instant!"

"But Sugar and Spice are Old Bessie's mascots. They *must* ride in the cab!" argued Mrs. Jepson.

"No way! It's far too dangerous," Jim said sternly. "Why do you think Skip has stayed behind in one of the coaches, instead of riding up front with me?"

"But my doggies are little. They can't possibly get in the way," pleaded Mrs. Jepson.

"Oh, come *on!*" Neil muttered under his breath. Trust Mrs. Jepson to cause yet another holdup. From inside the train, someone started to call out, "Why are we waiting?" Everyone aboard Old Bessie was getting fed up now. This delay was starting to spoil the day.

"You and Sugar and Spice are *not* traveling in the cab, and that's final!" Jim insisted, trying hard not to raise his voice. "Take them away, or this train's going nowhere!"

He and Mrs. Jepson glared at each other. Finally, Mrs. Jepson tossed her blond ringlets. "Oh, all *right!*" She passed Sugar and Spice down to Neil, who struggled to keep the excitable little terriers under control, then clambered down from the cab herself. Neil put the Westies gently down on the ground and handed Mrs. Jepson their leashes.

Mrs. Jepson strode back along the platform, her high heels clicking and Sugar and Spice barking every step of the way. She climbed into the front coach and Neil heard her boasting, "I've worked out the problem. We're going now!"

There was an outburst of excited cheering and someone started singing, "Here we go, here we go, here we go!" Voices joined in from all over the train, to the accompaniment of some enthusiastic barking.

Neil leaned out of the cab. His father was still on the platform with Jim. "What happens now?" Neil asked them.

"The hand-brake's off and she's ready to go," said Jim. "All I have to do now is make contact with Colin. He'll wave a flag and blow a whistle to tell me that it's safe to go, then I'll blow *my* whistle to confirm that I got his instructions. Then we jump on board. Got it?"

"Got it," said Bob.

With one foot on the step and the other on the platform, Jim looked down the length of the train. Neil stood on the foot-plate and followed his gaze. Colin blew three loud blasts, and a moment later Neil glimpsed two white streaks jump out of a carriage window, onto the platform. Jim obviously hadn't seen them, and blew his whistle as the white streaks raced toward him. Two small dogs hurled themselves at the engine, and Jim Brewster stumbled over them and fell onto the platform as they charged past him up the steps and into the cab.

Neil tripped over Spice, fell against a lever, and caught hold of another to save himself. There was a deafening hiss of steam, a chuffing sound, and, to his horror, the engine started to move.

"Jim, Dad! Get in, quick!" Neil yelled out of the cab window, his heart racing. He saw Jim scramble to his feet and make a lunge for the rail of the tender, but the train gave a jerk and his fingers slipped off the smooth metal.

"Neil! Hang on!" shouted Bob, sprinting down the platform. But the track was on a downhill slope and the train was gathering speed. Neil could see that his dad wouldn't catch up. Worse still, the words of instruction that Jim was yelling were drowned out by the hissing of the steam and the rhythmic clatter of the wheels.

Neil was in the cab of a train that was speeding uncontrollably down the track without a driver. His only companions were two disobedient dogs — who, he now noticed, didn't even have on their leashes anymore. Old Bessie's cargo of friends, family, and dogs was in serious danger. . . .

CHAPTER EIGHT

Neil stared around the cab and desperately tried to remember what Dan had told him about the controls. But in his state of panic his mind had gone blank. He pulled carefully on one of the levers, but it seemed to have no effect. He was scared to move any of the wheels or levers too much in case he brought the train to an abrupt halt and caused an accident. Old Bessie had to be stopped smoothly — but she seemed to be picking up speed with every passing second. *If only the line to Padsham didn't run downhill!* he thought desperately. Above the thunderous roar and clatter of the iron wheels, Neil was sure that he could hear alarmed shouts from the passengers in the coaches behind him. He just hoped that Jake was all right.

Neil wasn't quite tall enough to see out of the cab's small, round windows. To see ahead, he had to stick his head out of a side window, but when he did so, the wind tore through his hair, and smoke and smut half-blinded him. It was terrifying to see the landscape flying by so quickly. Neil tugged the chain that operated the whistle. At least that might reassure the passengers that there was someone in the cab. But it was a mistake. The hooting sound frightened Sugar and Spice. They leaped up and started tearing around the cab, yapping loudly.

"Sugar, Spice, sit!" commanded Neil sternly. But the little dogs refused to obey him. Spice stood on his hind legs and clawed at Neil's jeans. Without their leashes, there was no way of tethering them to anything, and Neil was terrified that they might jump up at the swing doors and fall out. Reluctantly, he latched the doors shut, hoping he wouldn't need to jump out in a hurry.

The train rattled around a bend and gave a sudden jolt that sent the two small terriers skittering into a corner. Sugar whimpered in fright, Spice licked her nose, and then the terrified Westies huddled together. Neil hoped they would stay still. His priority had to be stopping the train, not trying to control Sugar and Spice.

By now, Old Bessie seemed to be traveling at breakneck speed. Once again, Neil studied the controls and tried to think clearly. Was that brass wheel one of the brakes? But, as before, his mind went blank and he began to panic. He doubted that there was anyone else on board who could drive a steam train. And even if there was, it would be impossible for them to get to him, because there was no connecting door between the coaches and the engine. To reach the cab, someone would have to do what he'd only seen done in films — climb out of the window and crawl along the roof.

Neil had to face facts — he was truly alone, in charge of a runaway train. People's lives depended on him. It was a terrifying responsibility. Suddenly, his mind began to clear, and Dan's instructions started to come back to him. To stop a train you had to cut the amount of steam getting to the pistons, by pulling the regulator lever closed, then working the brake. Neil studied the controls. He remembered that the regulator had been on Dan's right. It had to be the lever he had fallen against when he tripped over Sugar and Spice — but he'd knocked it upward, out of his reach.

If only he had something to stand on . . . He looked around and saw a red bucket full of sand. Quickly, he emptied it out and turned the bucket upside down. The clanging noise startled the two Westies. Spice got to his feet and bounded toward Neil, banging into the bucket just as Neil was about to stand on it.

"*No*, Spice!" he shouted. The Westie looked bewildered. He was trembling, with his tail between his legs. He slunk back to Sugar, who was still in the corner, crouched behind a pipe.

Neil climbed onto the overturned bucket and reached for the regulator lever. He pulled the lever down toward him this time, afraid to do it quickly in case the train slowed down too suddenly. But the ground was sloping downward again and the train's own weight was carrying it faster and faster down the hill. Only someone who really knew what they were doing could stop Old Bessie now. Panic mounted in him. Glancing out of the window of the cab, Neil could see Padsham station drawing closer. They were thundering toward it at a frightening speed.

He knew he should work the whistle again, to warn people waiting to board at Padsham that Old Bessie was approaching. But he also knew that the shrill, deafening blast would upset the two Westies. He had to take the risk. He tugged hard on the chain several times, hoping people would realize that something was wrong. Sugar jumped up from her hiding place, ran to the doors, and scrabbled at them with her front paws, desperately trying to escape from the noises that hurt her sensitive ears. Spice threw back his head and howled.

As the engine rushed through the station, Neil saw surprise, then alarm, on people's faces. In a flash, he saw Mr. Hamley, with his wife and baby, and Dotty, their Dalmatian. They stared in amazement as Old Bessie hurtled past.

Neil pulled the regulator lever again — harder this time. There was a deafening hiss and, to his relief, he actually felt the engine slow down a little. Or was it just that he was at the foot of a hill now, and the track had started to climb up toward Colshaw? If *only* he could stop the train! He had no idea how to find the brake among the many wheels and levers, and he didn't have much longer to figure it out. Soon, the train would be nearing Colshaw Station, where the branch line came to an end. If the train hit the buffers, there would be a terrible accident. . . .

Don't panic! he told himself severely. The engine lurched to the left, around a bend in the track. Neil was sweating in the heat from the glowing firebox. His forehead was streaming. He lifted up the front of his T-shirt and wiped his face.

Suddenly, he realized that if *he* was hot and thirsty, the Westies must be desperate. Quickly, he reached for his backpack and felt for the water bottle. As he did so, his fingers closed around something else. His father's cell phone! If only he'd remembered it before!

The display screen said that there were five missed calls. Neil wasn't sure how to retrieve the numbers and there was no time to try. Instead, he dialed 911.

"Police, Compton area. Quick as you can," he told the control center urgently, shouting above the noise of the train. Moments later, he was connected. He was worried that they wouldn't believe him when he said he was in the cab of a runaway train, but they seemed to know all about it. "I need to contact Jim Brewster on his cell phone so he can tell me how to stop the train," Neil shouted urgently.

The police officer who had taken the call sounded very calm. "I'll find Jim Brewster's number and get him to call you," the officer said briskly. "Hang up now and don't worry." But Neil did worry. How could he help it when the train was getting closer and closer to Colshaw? At least it wasn't racing now, like it had been before. The firebox wasn't glowing quite

so brightly, either. *Perhaps it's running out of coal,*
Neil thought hopefully.

At last, the phone rang and Neil heard Jim Brewster's voice.

"Now, stay clam, do what I tell you, and everything
will be fine," Jim said, after Neil had reassured the
railway-man that he was OK. "There should be some
signals coming up soon. Look out for them and as
soon as you get near, I want you to do the following
things, in this order . . ."

Neil looked out and spotted the signals just in
time. He followed Jim's instructions carefully and,
by the time Colshaw Station came into sight, he had
slowed the giant engine right down.

"That's better," Jim said. "You can relax now. The
lower lever on your left will stop her altogether. I'll
tell you when to push it."

"Where are you?" Neil asked Jim.

"On the train," Jim replied.

"Is Dad on it, too?" said Neil.

"Yes. He's with Emily and Jake," the railway-man
said. "No more questions now. You've got to stop
the engine before we reach the end of the platform.
Pull the left-hand lever halfway down. That's the
brake . . . good. A bit more now . . . and shut off the
regulator."

As the noise of the train died down, Neil began to
hear dogs barking in the coaches behind him. Sugar
and Spice barked back. The two Westies looked

much happier now that the train was nearly at a standstill. Their ears were cocked and their stumpy tails were wagging.

"OK. Push the brake all the way," said Jim. "And . . . we're there!"

CHAPTER NINE

Neil was greeted by a roar that had nothing to do with the engine or the wind this time. It was the sound of people shouting, cheering, and clapping. Neil opened the swing doors and Sugar and Spice jumped down onto the platform. He followed them on shaky legs, feeling dazed.

"My darlings!" shouted Mrs. Jepson, rushing toward her dogs. She picked up the Westies and buried her tear-streaked face in their fur. "I was so worried," she told Neil. "I thought they might have fallen under the train! Thank you for keeping them safe."

People crowded around Neil, asking questions, but all he wanted to do was find his dad and Emily, and make sure Jake was all right. He was worried that all the commotion might have upset the Border collie.

Suddenly, there was a flurry of black-and-white fur and Jake was jumping up and licking him. "You were amazing," Emily called, pushing her way through the crowd of dogs and people, closely followed by Bob.

"I'm just glad it's all over," said Neil, laughing with relief and making a huge fuss over Jake. "It must have been hot in that carriage. Have you given him some water?" he asked Emily.

"Yes," she replied. "He's had lots."

"How did you and Jim manage to get on the train, Dad?" asked Neil.

"Someone held a carriage door open and pulled us in. I knew you had my cell phone and we called and called you on Jim's phone, but you didn't answer," said Bob. "I was really starting to panic."

Neil bit his lip. "It was my fault," he said. "I forgot I had your phone. It was in my backpack on the floor, and the train was so noisy I didn't hear it ring."

Just then, Sergeant Moorhead made his way through the crowds toward them, with his magnificent German shepherd, Sherlock, by his side. Jake wagged his tail in friendly greeting and the two young dogs touched noses.

"Sergeant Moorhead!" cried Emily. "We thought you were on vacation."

"I got back late last night," explained the sergeant. "You did a great job there, Neil. I need to ask you some questions, though, to find out exactly how this incident happened. I don't need to tell you how serious it could have been. Now, tell me how the train managed to set off without Jim Brewster in the driver's cab."

"Jim wasn't even supposed to be driving. Dan Cooper was the driver, but he disappeared," Neil said.

The sergeant nodded. "He's been found. Apparently, he got locked in the staff bicycle shed at Compton Station. No one knows how it happened. Debbie, the ticket clerk, heard him banging and shouting after the train had left."

"That's not the only odd thing that's happened," Neil remarked, and told the sergeant about all of the strange events of the previous week.

When he explained about Sugar and Spice getting loose, Sergeant Moorhead frowned. "It was precisely to prevent such an accident that the steam train committee decided that all dogs should be kept on leashes. Mrs. Jepson, of all people, should have known that," he said severely. "I think we need a few questions answered, don't you?"

Neil looked over at Mrs. Jepson, but she didn't seem aware of anything apart from Sugar and Spice. She was busy making a fuss over them and feeding them dog treats.

Sergeant Moorhead held up his hand for silence, then addressed the crowd. "I'm sure I don't need to remind you all that what happened today could have been a major catastrophe," he said. "It was only thanks to Neil Parker that Old Bessie arrived safely."

Neil felt his face redden as people cheered and clapped again.

"But all of this could have been avoided in the first place if some people had behaved more responsibly." The sergeant looked pointedly at Mrs. Jepson, who lowered her eyes when she saw his stern expression. "Why in the world did you let Sugar and Spice off their leashes, Mrs. Jepson?"

"But I didn't!" Mrs. Jepson insisted. "I don't know what happened. My husband was looking after them . . ." She turned to Mr. Jepson, who cleared his throat awkwardly.

"It had nothing to do with me, either" he said defensively. "I was still holding their leashes when they ran off. Someone must have unclipped them."

"And who would have done that?" asked Sergeant Moorhead impatiently.

"It was obviously Mrs. Jepson. Who else could it have been?" said a familiar voice behind Neil. He turned to see Mrs. Maitland-Smith, with Jemima at her feet. She spoke loudly, obviously intending everyone to hear.

The crowd stared at Mrs. Jepson. "It wasn't me!" she snapped, looking angry and upset now.

"Oh, come on! You just couldn't stand the thought of your little darlings being on leashes all day, could you? You spoil those dogs rotten — and just look how badly behaved they are!"

There was a murmur of agreement from the crowd. Mrs. Maitland-Smith obviously loved having an audience.

"If I tell *my* dog to stay, she stays. Don't you, Jemima?" she said.

The black poodle had been staring curiously at another dog. But, hearing her name, she sprang up to lick her owner's hand. As she did so, Mrs. Maitland-Smith's handbag fell to the floor, its contents spilling everywhere. Neil, who was nearest, bent down to gather up her belongings.

Jake decided to help, too. He picked up a small plastic bag in his teeth, dropped it at Neil's feet, then gave a loud sneeze. "Thanks, boy," Neil said, reaching for it. He was about to hand it to Mrs. Maitland-Smith when he noticed Jake licking his lips as if he had a nasty taste in his mouth. Neil looked more closely at the white flakes inside the bag and undid the wire tie securing it. He sniffed, and a strong, soapy smell promptly made him sneeze.

"Laundry detergent? What a strange thing to carry in your handbag!" he exclaimed.

Mrs. Maitland-Smith turned pale. She looked around anxiously, as if searching for the best escape route.

What's gotten into her? thought Neil. *What did I say?*

Then he remembered. Mike Turner had found laundry detergent on Sugar's fur. Could that have had something to do with Mrs. Maitland-Smith? She certainly looked guilty enough . . . But surely she wouldn't have tried to poison Sugar? She might not be Mrs. Jepson's greatest fan, but she *was* a dog lover.

Neil's mind was racing. He couldn't quite believe that she would be capable of harming Sugar, but the evidence pointed toward her. He decided to say something.

"Sugar was poisoned with laundry detergent," he began, watching her face closely. When he saw her guilty expression, he knew he was right. He was shocked — and Mrs. Jepson was furious. For once, she was speechless as she stared at Mrs. Maitland-Smith. She clutched the two little Westies to her chest.

"Some brands of laundry detergent contain chemicals that could kill a small animal!" Neil said angrily.

"I know that. That's why I was very careful about the brand I chose," Mrs. Maitland-Smith said defensively. "I just wanted to make one of the dogs a little bit sick, not kill her!"

The crowd began to mutter angrily. Sergeant Moorhead held up his hand for silence again.

"But why did you do it?" asked Bob Parker, mystified.

Mrs. Maitland-Smith glanced nervously at Mrs. Jepson. "I wanted this event to be mine," she said. "I knew that if one of Mrs. Jepson's dogs was ill, she would never leave her. She'd stay away from Old Bessie, and I'd be in charge. I should have been in charge in the first place," she added bitterly.

"So you put a dog's life in danger just for that?" asked Neil incredulously.

Mrs. Maitland-Smith looked down at her feet.

"How did you get Sugar to eat the laundry detergent?" asked Emily.

"I disguised the taste with liver," she said, sounding really sorry now. "It's got a strong flavor, so I knew it would hide the soapy taste. I cut a slit in it and sprinkled a little powder inside —"

"You did it when you came over for the committee meeting, didn't you?" interrupted Mrs. Jepson, finding her voice at last. "You nasty woman! You could have killed my dogs. You deserve to be locked up! You're not fit to own a dog."

Neil saw Mrs. Maitland-Smith stroke Jemima's head gently, as if to show how much she cared for the poodle. But Mrs. Jepson hadn't finished yet.

"I bet it was you who let poor Sugar and Spice off their leashes, too!" she accused angrily.

Mrs. Maitland-Smith bit her lip. "I'm sorry. Really I am," she said. "I only wanted them to be a bit of a nuisance and get in everybody's way, to make you look foolish."

"Sugar and Spice could have fallen under the wheels and been killed!" exclaimed Mrs. Jepson.

"I'm sorry, I'm really sorry," Mrs. Maitland-Smith said again, her eyes filling with tears. "I didn't mean to put anybody's life in danger and I didn't mean to hurt Sugar. I love dogs! I never meant to make her so ill — just a bit under the weather, to spoil your day," she added, flushing as she looked at Mrs. Jepson.

"You put over sixty people and their dogs at risk, just because of a petty rivalry?" Sergeant Moorhead said in amazement. There were murmurs of agreement all around.

"But I didn't mean to!" Mrs. Maitland-Smith insisted. "It never crossed my mind that anything like this could happen," she went on. "I thought the trip would be canceled when the driver didn't show up."

"I suppose that had something to do with you, too!" Dan Cooper glared at her.

Mrs. Maitland-Smith was silent.

"Well, it's not like I locked myself in the shed, did I?" snapped Dan.

"I just couldn't resist," said Mrs. Maitland-Smith at last, staring at the ground in embarrassment. "How was I to know that anyone else was qualified to drive the train? I was horrified when it started to move. Jemima and I were on it, too, remember?"

Neil thought of all the other strange events over the past week. It looked as if Mrs. Maitland-Smith was at the bottom of the mystery. She was the very last person Neil would have suspected of trying to sabotage the Puppy Express. After all, it was to raise funds for a memorial for her own grandmother's dog.

"Do you know anything about Jim's gold paint and stencils going missing?" he challenged her. "Or the mysterious phone calls to the printer's and the *Compton News*?"

Mrs. Maitland-Smith grimaced and shrugged. "Yes," she said quietly. "I just wanted to make Mrs. Jepson look incompetent. I thought she deserved it."

"And what about Marcus Welham?" Emily put in. "Can you explain what he was doing going on vacation?"

"I called his manager and told him the event had been canceled," Mrs. Maitland-Smith admitted guiltily.

"You just wanted to be the center of attention and open the Puppy Express yourself, didn't you?" said Mrs. Jepson.

The two women glared at one another, and Sergeant Moorhead stepped in between them.

"This is a serious matter, Mrs. Maitland-Smith," he said. "I'm afraid you're going to have to come down to the station to make a statement. It will be up to private individuals and the railway authorities to decide whether to press any charges."

"*I've* got a good mind to!" Mrs. Jepson sobbed. "I've never done her any harm and neither have Sugar

and Spice. She put our lives and my reputation at
risk. I worked very hard to make today a success. I
didn't deserve this — and my poor little darlings
certainly didn't!" She was still clutching the Westies
against her. Spice gave a little whimper and licked
her chin. Tears rolled down Mrs. Jepson's face and
Mr. Jepson hugged her awkwardly. Neil felt a wave
of sympathy for Mrs. Jepson. He could hardly blame
her for her reaction. He couldn't imagine how furious he would be if someone tried to poison Jake.

As Sergeant Moorhead put his hand on Mrs.
Maitland-Smith's shoulder to guide her toward his
car, a deep growl rumbled in Sherlock's throat.
Jemima gave a frightened yelp and backed off as far
as she could. Neil realized that the German shepherd was trained to guard his handler while arrests
were being made.

"It's all right, Sherlock," said the sergeant, giving
his dog a pat.

"I don't want to take Jemima to the station with
me," said Mrs. Maitland-Smith. "Bob, do you think
you could look after her?"

"No problem," said Bob.

"Thank you. I'll pick her up from King Street when
the sergeant's finished with me. There you are,
Jemima. You be a good girl now." She handed the
poodle's leash to Bob. Jemima pawed at her owner's
leg. The dog seemed to know that they were about to

be parted and was getting agitated. Bob stroked the poodle and talked to her soothingly.

"Don't worry. We'll make sure she's very well cared for," said Neil, bending down to ruffle the poodle's curls.

After the police car had left, people milled around and chatted, excited by the drama but not quite sure what to do next. Mrs. Jepson made a valiant effort, dried her tears, and took charge.

"Now that our real driver is here" — she gestured toward Dan Cooper — "anyone who would like to travel back to Compton on old Bessie should take their seats now."

"Hurrah!" cheered the crowd.

"I wouldn't blame you if you didn't want to go back on the train, Neil," Emily said.

"Of course I do!" Neil laughed. "Come on, Jake. I'd like to sit with you in comfort, as a passenger this time, though. Traveling in the cab is a little too scary!"

When they arrived back at Compton, Bob offered to drive Hasheem and Rehana home.

"I couldn't fit the Range Rover in the parking garage, so I parked on Fernlea Drive," said Bob. "I hope you don't mind a short walk."

Fernlea Drive was a hilly road, lined with detached bungalows. As they went to cross over to where their car was parked, a red convertible pulled out of a parking space farther up the street.

"Just look at that! He's gabbing away on his cell phone and not looking where he's going," Bob complained. "Talk about careless —"

"Dad!" Emily screamed, covering her face with her hands.

"No!" yelled Neil at the top of his voice. They had both seen the brown-and-white spaniel dashing out of a garden, right into the path of the oncoming car.

CHAPTER TEN

The spaniel stood in the middle of the road, paralyzed with fright. Hasheem was the first to react. He sprinted into the road, snatched up the dog, and swerved back out of the car's path — not a second too soon. There was a screech of brakes and the convertible came to a sudden stop.

The driver wound down his window. "Hey, kid! Why don't you look where you're going?" he shouted.

Bob Parker stepped forward. "Excuse *me*, but I think it's *you* who wasn't looking where you were going!" he said angrily. "You were on the phone — you weren't paying attention. You could have killed that dog, not to mention us!"

The man apologized sheepishly and drove off at a

much slower speed. Hasheem gently set the trembling spaniel on the ground. Neil crouched down to inspect its collar, then looked up with an amazed expression. "It's Pauline Ford's dog, Poppy!" he said. "Pauline's the one with the puppy that Mr. Hamley told us about," he explained to his dad.

"Oh, she's beautiful," Rehana sighed, stroking the trembling dog. "Do you think her puppy looks like her?"

"She probably does," Neil replied.

Just then, Pauline Ford came dashing out of her house. The young woman looked shocked as she rushed up to Poppy and made a huge fuss over her.

"I saw it all from an upstairs window. I thought Poppy had been killed!" she said in a wobbly voice. "The gardener must have left the gates open. Is she all right?"

"Don't worry, Poppy's fine," Neil reassured her, stroking the dog's silky ears. "I'm Neil Parker, by the way." He introduced everyone, and Pauline Ford held out a shaking hand to Hasheem. "You saved Poppy's life," she said emotionally. "What can I do to thank you?"

Rehana smiled brightly at her. "Could you let us see Poppy's puppy?" she asked.

Pauline laughed. "Of course you can!" she said. "I guess you must all go to Meadowbank School."

"That's right," Emily confirmed.

"I'll stay here with Jake and Jemima," said Bob. "All these strange dogs in the house might be too much for a little puppy."

Pauline Ford led them into a bright, cozy kitchen. On the rug was an adorable puppy. She was playing with a piece of wrapping paper, biting and tearing it to shreds. Like her mother, the puppy was brown-and-white, with pretty tan spots on her chest and muzzle, and big furry ears. Rehana went straight over to her. "Can I pet her?" she asked.

"Of course!" Pauline smiled. "Excuse me a moment," she said, and left the room.

Hasheem joined his sister, and kneeled down beside the little spaniel. Poppy immediately stepped in front of her puppy, as if to protect her, and sniffed Hasheem's and Rehana's fingers. Obviously deciding they were no threat, she jumped up onto the couch and settled down to sleep.

Neil watched Rehana stroke the puppy's silky tummy as she lay on her back with her paws in the air. Then the puppy curled herself around Rehana and licked her hand. The little girl looked totally smitten. Pauline came back into the room and handed Rehana a red rubber squeaky toy. She showed it to the spaniel, who snatched it in her mouth, eager for a game of tug-of-war. "I could play with her all day!" Rehana said, her eyes shining.

"She's great," said Hasheem. He stroked the pup,

too, laughing when she playfully kicked at his hand. "Have you thought of a name yet?" he asked.

Pauline Ford shook her head. "No. It will be up to the new owner to choose one."

"If I had her, I'd call her Bessie, after that brave retriever," Rehana said longingly.

"That's a great idea!" said Emily.

Rehana lay down on the carpet next to the pup and giggled as the little spaniel licked her face. Hasheem looked at the pair of them, an anxious expression on his face. Neil knew that he was worried that his sister was getting too attached to the spaniel.

"Come on, Rehana, we should go now," he told her. "Mom will be wondering where we are."

The said good-bye to Pauline Ford, Poppy, and the little puppy, and piled into the car. As Bob was driving them home, Hasheem said, "I suppose we've got to face the fact that we might not get her. Our project may not be the best."

"Of course it is," said Rehana confidently. "Anyway, I know we'll get Bessie, 'cause I made a wish on Sarah's four-leaf clover."

Neil and Hasheem exchanged glances and grins, but Neil saw that Hasheem had his fingers crossed. He could tell that his friend wanted the puppy just as much as his little sister did.

"Neil! There's someone here to see you," called Carole Parker. Neil was eating a cheese sandwich in the kitchen, ravenous after the day's excitement. Cramming the last of it into his mouth, he went to see who was at the door. To his surprise, he found Mr. and Mrs. Jepson there, with Sugar and Spice.

"We came to say thank you, Neil," mumbled Mr. Jepson. "I don't know what we would have done without you. If you hadn't kept your head, we might not be standing here now."

"And thank you for taking such good care of Sugar and Spice," Mrs. Jepson added.

Spice jumped up at Neil, demanding his attention. Jake, who had padded down the hallway after Neil, looked down at Sugar, who started racing around the Border collie and barking wildly.

"My husband's got something else to tell you," prompted Mrs. Jepson, nudging Mr. Jepson.

The tall, grumpy-looking councillor gave one of his rare smiles. "As a way of saying thanks for what you did, I'm making a large personal donation to Bessie's memorial fund in your name, Neil. With that, and today's ticket proceeds and other donations, we've got more than enough to pay for the memorial and the restoration of more coaches for the steam train."

"That's great!" said Neil. But before he had a chance to say anything else, he caught sight of a blue car being parked in the courtyard, behind the Jepsons' Volvo. Mr. and Mrs. Jepson turned around to see what Neil was staring at, and their friendly expressions turned to stony glares. Mrs. Maitland-Smith got out of the car and started walking toward them.

"We'll be going now," Mr. Jepson told Neil. Mrs. Jepson hastily gathered up Sugar and Spice in her arms, but she was too late. Mrs. Maitland-Smith stepped right in front of her.

"I was just coming for Jemima, but I'm glad I caught you, Mrs. Jepson," she said. "I want to apologize to you. I behaved very childishly. I've made statements to both the police and the *Compton News*, and given a public apology. No one will think you were to blame for anything."

Neil watched the two women closely. Mrs. Maitland-

Smith seemed genuinely sorry for what she'd done, but Mrs. Jepson's expression was still hostile and she was clutching Sugar and Spice so tightly that the little dogs were squirming.

"I especially want to say sorry for what I did to Sugar. I don't know what I was thinking. I love dogs, and she's a gorgeous little thing." Mrs. Maitland-Smith reached a tentative hand toward Sugar, who licked her fingers.

Mrs. Jepson's face softened slightly. "I think Sugar's forgiven you," she said. "But it may take me a bit longer, I'm afraid."

"I understand," said Mrs. Maitland-Smith quietly.

The Jepsons left quickly and Neil led Mrs. Maitland-Smith to the pen where Jemima had been housed temporarily. Emily was sitting with Jemima, hugging her. The poodle was resting her front paws on Emily's shoulders and was trying to lick her nose.

"She's such a friendly dog!" Emily laughed, wiping her face with her hand.

"Yes, she's got a lovely temperament," Mrs. Maitland-Smith agreed. "Thanks for looking after her. And Neil, as a way of saying sorry to you and your family for everything I put you through, I'd like to invite you all to come up to the stables some day soon and have a free ride."

"It's a kind offer, but I think we're more of a dog family, really," Emily said, looking at Neil. They couldn't imagine their parents wanting them to have anything to do with Mrs. Maitland-Smith for a long time.

As Jemima and her owner left, both of them happy to be back in the other's company, Jake ran out to meet Neil.

"Come on, time for your evening walk," he told the collie.

As they climbed the steep hill that led up to the park, Neil thought about the day's events. He was exhausted, but pleased with the way things had turned out. There was just one thing that was worrying him. Tomorrow, Mr. Hamley would announce the name of the person whose project was the best. Neil was desperately hoping that Hasheem and Rehana would win, and that the springer spaniel pup would be theirs.

"You're a very lucky boy, Jake," Neil told his Border collie, who had a stick in his mouth and was pestering Neil to throw it for him. "You're not like Rusty's pups, or Poppy's pup. There was never any doubt about who was going to own *you*. Now fetch!"

Neil hurled the stick as far as he could, and Jake raced after it, excited by the fresh air and the open space after the confinement and noise of that afternoon.

Neil hardly dared look at Hasheem the next morning as the pupils of Meadowbank School filed into the auditorium for assembly. He couldn't see Rehana from where he was sitting, but he could imagine how anxious she must have been feeling.

Mr. Hamley cleared his throat and looked around the auditorium.

"Now, I know you're all waiting to hear about Poppy's pup," he said, "and I'm afraid you're going to be disappointed by what I'm about to say . . ."

Neil glanced at Hasheem in alarm. *Don't say that Mrs. Ford's given Bessie to someone else*, he thought desperately.

Mr. Hamley continued. "The quality of the projects submitted was so high that we were unable to make a decision over the weekend. I'm going to have to ask you all to be patient for a little bit longer. Until lunchtime, to be precise, because I want Mrs. Sharpe to read them, too."

Hasheem gave a loud groan. "It's not fair!" he said quietly to Neil.

But Mr. Hamley had heard him. He nodded and said, "I'm sorry, but it's the best I can do. You must all assemble here again at two o'clock. I promise I'll give you our decision then."

The principal continued talking, but Neil scarcely heard a word he said. All he could think of was how hard it was on Hasheem and Rehana.

"How do they expect me to concentrate on school-work this morning?" Hasheem grumbled when the assembly was over.

"Why don't you pretend you're sick and go home?" suggested Chris Wilson with a grin.

"Because if I did that, I'd miss the announcement!" replied Hasheem. "I don't think I've got much of a chance, though — not if everyone's projects are so good." He sighed.

Neil did his best to distract his friend and take his mind off the terrible wait. In fact, he did too good a job and was reprimanded for talking during math. But at last it was quarter to two and Neil and Hasheem took their places in the school auditorium.

Mrs. Sharpe stood next to Mr. Hamley. They were both smiling.

"I won't keep you in suspense any longer," the head teacher said. "Three of us have read the projects now, and we have arrived at a very difficult decision. The students who we feel have given the most care to animals over the past year are . . ." he paused, and Neil couldn't tell where he was looking as his eyes swept the auditorium. "Hasheem and Rehana Lindon," he finally announced, and a huge cheer broke out.

Neil slapped Hasheem on the back. "Congratulations!" he said. "They couldn't have chosen better. Can I come with you when you go to get Bessie?"

"Sure!" said Hasheem, grinning widely.

When the noise had died down, Mr. Hamley cleared his throat, and this time his eyes singled out Neil. "I don't know if you're aware of it," he said, "but we have a hero among us. Neil Parker, come up to the front!"

Oh, no! thought Neil, blushing as he got to his feet and walked to the front of the auditorium. He had to stand there with all eyes on him as Mr. Hamley told the rest of the school about how he had stopped Old Bessie from crashing.

"I've been trying to think of a reward we could give you," the principal said.

"I don't want a reward," Neil replied. "But there is one thing . . ."

"What's that?" asked Mr. Hamley.

"Well, we've got a stray dog in the rescue center called Rusty, who's got four healthy puppies," explained Neil. "We need to find homes for them all. So I thought that those students who really want a dog

but weren't lucky enough to get the springer spaniel puppy might like to come over to King Street Kennels and have a look at them. . . ."

As Neil spoke, he was aware of an undercurrent of laughter. Soon, it filled the auditorium. Even Mr. Hamley was laughing.

"What's wrong?" asked Neil, feeling even more embarrassed.

Mr. Hamley held up his hand for silence. "Nothing's wrong," he said. "Can't you guess what everyone's thinking? That the Puppy Patrol has lived up to its name yet again!"